GRAY COURT

HAILEY EDWARDS

This is a work of fiction. Names, characters, businesses, places, events and incidents are either the products of the author's imagination or used in a fictitious manner. Any resemblance to actual persons, living or dead, or actual events is purely coincidental.

Edited by Sasha Knight
Copy Edited by Kimberly Cannon
Proofread by Lillie's Literary Services
Cover by Damonza
Illustration by NextJenCo

GRAY COURT

Black Hat Bureau, Book 7

After wiping out an entire black witch coven on the shores of Lake Pontchartrain, Rue can no longer afford to have a laissez-faire attitude toward the Maudit Grimoire. Its black magic is infecting her, and it's leaking into her familiar bond with Colby, poisoning the loinnir with its thirst for violence.

A trip to the fae realm ought to be just the ticket, but any hope for a quick fix dies when a message arrives from High Priestess Naeema. Her daughter has gone missing, and she tasks Rue with finding her in exchange for her help. With the grimoire sinking its hooks in deeper, can Rue afford to put off disposing of the cunning book yet again? The price of saving Naeema's daughter might cost Rue her own.

CHAPTER ONE

"*I* can't decide how to fill the eggs."

Lashes matted together with sleep, I groaned and rolled onto my stomach, mashing my face into my pillow. No. That was the whole problem. It wasn't *my* pillow. It was a *new* pillow. A *fluffy* pillow. Stuffed with a hypoallergenic down alternative, whatever that meant.

Its plush extravagance left me aching for the lumpy pancake I had been sleeping on for years, but that pillow—*my* pillow—was at home. A home that might as well have been on another planet compared to the farm and the tiny house where Asa and I now lived as a result of my falling out with Camber and Arden. The same tiny house that had suffered a seasonally challenged golem incursion before dawn.

"I bought six dozen multicolor plastic eggs, one dozen plastic gold eggs, and one giant grand prize egg."

Groping for Asa's ridiculously soft pillow, I snatched it and covered my head, sandwiching my ears between two luxurious golem-muffling layers.

"The colored ones are easy." He ignored my attempts to ignore him. "I put gift cards for local restaurants in those."

The mattress dipped when he invited himself to sit beside me, and

I rolled toward him, wrapping myself in the comforter like a breakfast burrito.

Mmm.

Smoked beef brisket, molten cheese, fried potatoes, scrambled eggs, with tomatillo sauce on a homemade tortilla. Throw in a few green chilies, and you had perfection.

Now *that* would have gotten me out of bed with a smile on my face.

"The gold ones are giving me fits." He shifted his weight closer. "What's better than the gift of food?"

The gift of sleep.

"Go away." I snuggled down until the covers brushed my nose. "The sun isn't up yet."

"You mean that great burning ball of hydrogen and helium that has no respect for the melting point of wig adhesive? That was up hours ago." He turned smug. "So was Ace."

That cracked my eyelids open, as he knew it would. I squinted at the khaki sunhat he sported to protect his bare scalp from sunburn. A wig would have helped with that, but no. Clay's paranoia over bleaching his babies meant he preferred to go au naturel on the farm.

"I had blackout shutters installed on all the windows." He leaned over and mashed buttons on a digital display Colby had explained away as the brains of the operation. Thermostat. Fuse box. Solar panels. Voice commands for lights and music trained to respond to Asa and not me after she caught me barking orders into thin air with increasingly violent tones one too many times. "Let there be light."

Wide slats within the double-pane windows fanned out like blinds then cranked up into a decorative recess, allowing for golden sunlight to bathe my unimpressed face.

"Ugh." I kept burrowing until the fabric covered my head, but it was too thin to do much good. "Argh."

"I believe the word you're looking for is *arrr*." He yanked, exposing my tender eyeballs again. "As in *arrr, maties*."

"The word I'm looking for can't be said in polite company."

"We have company?" He glanced left to right, up and down, front to back. "I don't see anyone."

"Well, at least you know I didn't mean you." I gave up on rest and shoved upright, settling into a dejected slump against the padded headboard. "St. Patrick's Day is…" I could *not* math this early. "Let's say a week away." Easter jumped around, which made tallying days even harder. "That means your eggstravaganza is…" I tried picturing a calendar in my head with no luck, "…a month out?"

"Eggstravaganza is now mine." He dictated a note to his smart-watch. "I've co-opted it. Thank you."

"Religious reasons aside—" I folded my legs under me, resisting the temptation to stretch them out then slide slowly, slowly down until I was right back where I started from. "Actually, no. That's it." I wiped the corners of my eyes. "That's why the centuria doesn't hunt eggs. Not their circus, not their monkeys."

A bunny delivering chocolates to fake grass nests made about as much sense, theologically, as Santa shimmying down chimneys to leave gifts under artificial trees.

Good thing I didn't have to understand where the symbology went wrong to appreciate the commercialized versions of holidays.

"But egg hunts are *fun*." He made bunny ears behind his head. "The centuria needs more joy in their lives."

"You're building them a water park." I *never* wanted to see those bills. "That's all anyone needs."

"You hunt eggs with Colby."

"I didn't know what to do with a kid when she first came to live with me, so yes. I celebrated every holiday to make sure she didn't miss out on one that might have been important to her or her family."

The way Colby coped with her transformation into a moth was to pretend she had always had wings, that it had always been only the two of us, that she had sprung into existence the night she died at the hands of a serial killer who would have consumed her soul had she not chosen me as the lesser evil.

Those earliest bumbling attempts I made to ensure her happiness saddled us with a yoke of family traditions no self-respecting black witch would be caught dead honoring.

Good thing I was embracing my gray areas these days.

"She conned you into celebrating big gift holidays." Clay laughed proudly. "You realize that, don't you?"

"All the excess holiday cheer in our lives? She's not responsible. I am." I swung my legs over the edge of the mattress, unable to sit still while reliving those dark days. "I was terrified I would kill her with neglect. She was afraid I would cave to the temptation of consuming her magic." I rose and crossed to the nearest window. "We tiptoed around each other, barely spoke. It was miserable and awkward. Ugly sweaters, anatomically incorrect hearts, and gelatinous cranberry cylinders helped us bond when we had nothing else in common."

"Normally, I would advise the way to anyone's heart is through their stomach, but you can only dress up sugar water and pollen in so many ways."

"Agave nectar, evaporated cane juice, malt syrup, coconut sugar." That was just her liquid diet. "The list only gets worse from there."

Exotic pollen granules alone threatened to bankrupt me until Colby decided she preferred to eat local.

Having been born a fae child, she'd had to figure out her new dietary preferences as a moth.

Having been raised a black witch, I had to figure out how to break my chain of addiction to be present in her life. And, you know, not eat her.

Holidays were as good a way as any to bridge the gap between our past and ever-evolving present selves.

"Has Colby ever had competition for her egg hunt?"

"No." Through the window, I located Asa in dark wash jeans, a new wardrobe staple. His messy man bun begged me to pull the elastic free then comb out the tangles with my fingers. "There was no one else."

As the person who hid the eggs, I would have ended the hunt in minutes if I joined in.

"Think how much fun she'll have this year." He came up behind me. "She'll massacre the centuria."

"Then choose your grand prize appropriately," I advised him. "Let's keep it tangible, okay?"

Now that I paid her a salary, she had chests full of pixelated gold coins in her various Mystic Realms lairs. And armor, and potions, and weapons, and rideable creatures of various mythological origins.

Pretty much everything a girl could want on her quest to vanquish the orc scourge on land and sea.

"That I can do."

Knowing Clay, *tangible* meant *tech*, but I wanted her to spend quality time with her online friends too. It was good for her to bond with kids her own emotional age. Their playdates and sleepovers might occur within the digital landscape of their favorite game, but she didn't stick out among gamers. Most of them lived too far away to ever visit one another IRL, so they were content with being virtual besties.

Mornings like this one, where Clay stabbed me in the eye with the sun to wake me, I wouldn't mind being able to turn off a monitor to banish him while I slept in.

There were definite perks to having friends you could unplug for a few hours when you wanted alone time.

"Hmm." His voice went soft in thought. "I wonder if Mr. Squiggles would like an egg in his tank."

"Sure." I had no idea how jellyfish felt about plastic eggs, but they did float. "I bet he would love it."

Maybe it would remind him of the friends he left behind in Lake Pontchartrain.

"I agree." He grinned. "I have one almost his exact same color."

Things on the other side of the window got interesting, and I forgot all about the jellyfish.

"What is he doing?" I pressed my nose to the cool glass. "Why is he half naked?"

"Ace?" Clay peered over my shoulder. "He was sparring earlier."

Sweat. Bare skin. Violence.

Three of my favorite looks on him.

Peeling away from the view, I scowled back at my so-called bestie. "You woke me up for your eggsistential crisis, but not that?"

"Co-opting." He murmured a reminder of the word to his watch. "That is also now mine."

To get his attention, I thumped his ear, and my hand came back smelling like his sunscreen.

"Everyone is afraid of your temper after you almost killed Moran for giving him a boo-boo." He tweaked my nose as payback. "You've been banned from spectating until *after* you mate him."

"It was only the one time." I rubbed my nose, guaranteeing I would smell coconut all day. "I apologized to Moran."

"I notice you didn't promise to try harder to behave yourself."

"I can't imagine ever letting someone take a swing at him without retribution."

Fascination took the blame now, sure, but I worried I was just as much at fault for my protective streak.

"Hmm." He scratched his jaw. "We assumed this too would pass."

"Yes, well, you know what they say about when you assume."

It makes an ass out of u and me.

Eager to close the distance between me and Asa, specifically my tongue and his salty-sweet throat, I shoved Clay out the door and pulled on jeans and a tee. I skipped shoes, which sucked for my tender feet, but bare was best. With fresh dirt pressed between my toes, the earth would familiarize itself with my power signature quicker. Thanks to the sharp stones, I fed the land a few drops of blood every day as I walked it from corner to corner, laying a path that would become permanent wards over time.

The whole process felt like starting over from scratch. Home was *right there*, but I was stuck over here. Here wasn't a bad place to be, but it wasn't home. Home was a small white house on a hill with a stream behind it and friends living down the road.

Except, my memory helpfully supplied, Camber and Arden weren't my friends anymore.

One had yet to realize it, thanks to her choice to relinquish her memories, but the other…

Arden would never forget or forgive what I had done. Her decision to retain her memories guaranteed she would remember enough for the both of them.

Once I secured my new wand—fine, so it was a footlong round dowel stolen from Clay's crafting stash—I strapped on my kit of magical accoutrements. The pang of absence from my first wand left me heartsore and unmotivated to source wood for a new one.

Most wands required an emotional link to allow them to channel power.

For white witches, it was a familial element. For black witches, it was a link to an important death.

Mine, snipped off the magnolia tree that leaned over Mom's symbolic grave, had covered both bases.

But now, with her spirit wandering with Dad, her burial site felt emptier than ever.

Granted, a dowel wasn't an ideal conductor, but the link to Clay was enough to make it work.

Balanced on the top step leading down into our small communal yard, I paused to let my eyes adjust to the piercing sunlight.

Before I could blink, a white blur smacked me in the face, knocking me into the siding, and my skull cracked against the door. *"Oomph."*

"I win." Colby slapped my cheeks with excited wingbeats. "You're the slowest daemon on the planet."

Careful not to hurt her, I peeled her off and cuddled her to my chest. "I don't have brain damage, thanks for asking."

"Sorry," she panted, voice high and reedy. "I had to win, and you got in the way."

That was Clay logic if I ever heard it. Their unholy alliance continued to be the best and worst idea ever.

With her tucked in close, I shoved off the door with my shoulders. "Who are you tormenting today?"

"Pegleg."

Given the Mystic Seas obsession sweeping the farm, I couldn't begin to guess who had earned that nickname. "Who?"

"Me." A boy with stone-gray skin and silver-white hair trotted the final distance while Colby basked in her win. "I'm Peleg, milady." He waited for me to descend the stairs then took my hand, bowed over it, and kissed my knuckles. "It's a pleasure to meet you."

"And you." I refused to melt inside at his adorableness. "You must be new to the centuria."

"No, milady." A pale blush whitened his cheeks. "I've come to visit my mother."

"Ah." I hadn't realized security was allowing new faces on the property. "Who might that be?"

"Primipilus Moran."

A bolt of understanding struck me, and Clay's sudden obsession with his Eggstravaganza made a whole lot more sense.

This wasn't about the daemons. Okay, not *only* about them. This was about Moran. And impressing her kid. The way to a single mom's heart wasn't through her stomach, but through her child.

"Your mother is a fierce warrior." I itched to ruffle the hair around his tiny horns, imagining this must be how Asa looked while his were growing in. "I bet you're one too."

"I am too young for battle," he lamented, "but I will prove myself to Mother one day."

"I hope you're a better fighter than you are a runner," Colby sassed him. "I beat you four times."

"You have wings, Lady Moth." He offered her a shy smile. "How can I ever hope to catch you?"

"Practice," she laughed, and zoomed off to race him back to their starting point.

With a polite bow to me, Peleg loped after her, a slender tail tufted in white swishing behind him.

"Good morning." Asa kissed my nape, and I nearly jumped out of my skin. "I see you've met our guest."

The trauma of that interaction had dulled my senses if I hadn't noticed how the heat amplified the rich green apple and warm cherry tobacco scent of his skin sooner.

"That boy…" I gawked after them. "He was *flirting* with Colby."

"Why do you think I stayed to supervise?" His laughter puffed against my neck. "I hope you don't mind."

"The flirting?" I began mentally drafting an *if you hurt her, I will [fill in the blank]* speech. "I haven't decided yet."

Daemons came in all shapes and sizes, but I hadn't considered age a factor. It never crossed my mind that a child would view Colby as a peer and develop a crush. The impossibility of it hurt me, as if he had already broken her heart by moving on as he outgrew their friendship while time stood still for her.

"I meant that he's here." Sensing the turn of my mood, he wrapped his arms around me. "Moran was on patrol this morning and spotted him near the perimeter."

A chill swept up my spine, regardless of the warmth encasing my back. "How did he find us?"

"Moran wants to give him time, says he'll tell us when he's ready."

"And you're damned if you do, damned if you don't." He was dealing with a worried mom, not his battle-hardened Primipilus. He had to tread carefully with her to avoid issuing a direct order, one that ran counter to her natural inclinations, which was always a last resort. "Press Peleg, and she'll become defensive. Wait him out, and the farm is in security limbo."

If Peleg didn't crack soon, Asa would have no choice, and it would destroy her trust in him.

"Let's sic Colby on him." I leaned hard into Peleg's crush. "See if she can wheedle it out of him."

Kids were faster to talk to their friends than their parents. Especially if what they had to say would get them in trouble.

"She is an excellent wheedler." His lips twitched. "Probably from spending too much time with Clay."

"If that doesn't work, we go to Moran, and we get answers." I exhaled. "Who was watching him?"

"He was left with his father." He rested his chin on top of my head. "In Hael."

"Maybe it's a sticky custody agreement, and Peleg wanted to see his mother."

Except that didn't explain how he got here, or how he knew where *here* was unless she told him.

"That's the general consensus." Unease wove through his words, but we owed Moran the benefit of the doubt. "He's a brave boy. Resourceful. He's also, as you noticed, smitten with Colby."

"How do we know he wasn't sent to befriend her, lure her off the property, and surrender her to Stavros?"

"We don't." He didn't sugarcoat the truth for me. "That's why he's not going anywhere until we have verified answers."

"I want eyes on Colby at all times until Peleg goes home." I turned in his arms. "I don't want to stick my foot in it with Moran, but Colby is—"

"I know." He pressed his lips to my forehead. "She has a shadow, and so does he."

"Yet you stayed out here." I smoothed my hands over his damp shoulders. "Why?"

"I don't presume to make decisions on Colby's behalf for you." His eyes grew heavy-lidded as I skimmed down his arms to hold his elegant hands. "Moran sent for me as soon as she returned with Peleg. The commotion must have woken Colby. She beat me to them, and she spotted him immediately. I couldn't undo the damage, but I set precautions in place until you could be informed of the situation."

More than likely, she had been up gaming with her friends from overseas hours past her bedtime.

No doubt she heard the ruckus, climbed into the clear acrylic tubes joining our houses, saw another kid, and zoomed off to introduce herself as fast as her wings would carry her.

The worst part?

It was my own fault.

I was the one who gave her free run of the farm. I was the one who told her no one here would harm her. And now I was the one stuck evaluating her new friend for ulterior motives.

Shaking off my parental fears, I reassured Asa that he had done no wrong. "I trust you."

"Yes." He brought my hand to his cheek and nuzzled into my palm. "But this is Colby."

A thick knot of feeling—*ick*—clogged my throat, but I choked out the words. "I trust you...with Colby."

The admission cost me as much as telling him I loved him for the first time. Maybe more. There was no difference between placing my life in his hands and allowing him to cradle hers too. Her life and mine were knotted by the familiar bond. Cut one thread, and you sliced us both. But it was important for him to know, to hear me say, that I had faith he would protect her for herself. Not only for me.

"Thank you." He pressed soft kisses to my fingertips. "I know that was hard for you."

"I prefer when other things are hard for me." I slipped a finger past his lips, and my nail bumped the diamond stud piercing his tongue. "Perhaps you and I—?"

"Be gross later." Clay pried us apart with an elbow to each of our chests. "Look at this now."

"How do you always know," I wondered for the millionth time, "the worst possible moment to interrupt us?"

"We all have our gifts." He inserted himself between us. "But seriously." He held up a gold foil envelope. "I'm not cockblocking for funsies."

One of my eyebrows twitched at the harsh language, but Colby was off with Peleg, so no harm done. "Liar."

"We just had a supply drop." He aimed the words at me as he shoved the paper into Asa's hand. "This came for you, Ace."

The centuria were handling grocery and supply runs for the farm, using the simple tasks to practice blending in among humans, with varying degrees of success.

"Grandmother's seal." Asa smoothed his thumb over the golden wax circle imprinted with a blazing sun then lifted his gaze to mine. "We have our answer."

For my sake, he had petitioned his grandmother, High Priestess Naeema, for an audience. The hope was, since she made the Tinkkit choker for me, she might have a theory as to why I blacked out before reducing the entire Toussaint coven to ash on the shores of Lake Pontchartrain.

Granted, he went light on the details, in case the message was intercepted, to protect our secrets.

Like, oh, I don't know. How I locked the Maudit Grimoire inside a djinn's ruby. Or that his mother fastening the gift around my neck merged the Tinkkit choker and the others in as yet undetermined but deadly ways. That kind of information left a trail, and we couldn't risk anyone following it back to me.

That book could *not* fall into the wrong hands, and neither could I.

Not while some combination of the three was willing to mass murder to protect me.

"Are you sure about this?" I placed my hand on his before his thumb slid under the flap. "I don't want to make things worse for you."

The scandal of his conception had branded him an outcast, and his daemon blood condemned him in fae eyes. Bringing home a witch with my past to meet the family wouldn't do his reputation any favors.

"The worst is over." His lips hitched on one side. "I have you now."

And I would go Blay on them, twisting off heads like bottlecaps, before I let Asa's pride take a hit on my behalf.

"Give me that." Clay snatched it away and ripped it open. "We need an answer sometime today."

We only had so much time before the director would wonder where his heir apparent had disappeared to, and I couldn't afford to let him know why I was visiting the fae realm. If he discovered I had the grimoire, he wouldn't rest until he killed me for it. Whatever value I held paled in comparison to the collection of dark and deadly magic. Spells so lethal Dad wrote them down to purge himself of their foulness.

Which would have been nice to know *before* I turned the grimoire into a fashion accessory.

"There's good news, and there's bad news." A sharp line pinched Clay's forehead. "Which do you want to hear first?"

"Why not mix it up?" I elected to rip off the Band-Aid slower, certain it wouldn't hurt any less no matter what order he chose. "Tell us something good."

"Your presence has been requested at a bunch of squiggly letters I assume means *temple*."

"Temple?" I frowned at the change in venue. "I thought the goal was the fae court?"

"It was." A ripple twitched in Asa's jaw. "What's the bad news?"

"Your mother." Clay hesitated before passing the letter to him. "She's missing."

Without setting eyes on the page, Asa slipped the paper in his back pocket and strode off into the trees.

He didn't look back.

"Give him a minute." Clay offered me the envelope. "Let him wrap his head around this."

The letter was addressed to *Most Beloved Grandson*, but there were characters beneath those words I couldn't read.

"That's the family motto," Clay explained after noticing my confusion. *"To be rather than seem to be."*

"How could you read that, if you couldn't decipher the name of the temple?"

"How can I snoop through Ace's correspondence with impunity if he knows I'm fluent?"

Old as he was, I doubted a language existed that Clay didn't speak or at least read. "Any particular reason why you're snooping?"

"Stavros."

Cold dread swooped through my belly, and I was glad I hadn't eaten breakfast yet. "He wrote to Asa?"

"He's a king, Dollface." He rolled his eyes. "His secretary, Bartholomew, handles his correspondence."

"Okay, I'll bite." I already regretted playing along. "What does Bartholomew have to say?"

"Mew-Mew, as I like to think of him, says that Stavros is willing to advance Ace half his inheritance if Ace cedes all rights to you as his object of fascination."

"You should have let me sleep in." I pinched the bridge of my nose. "How did Asa respond?"

"He balled it up, smoothed it out, tore it into little pieces, then tossed it in a burn barrel." He tapped the side of his head. "See? Aren't you glad I snooped? Otherwise, we'd never know your fair market value."

"Yes. Thank you, Clay. I'll sleep better tonight knowing I'm worth more than a few cows or a fast horse."

"You're welcome," he said without a hint of guile.

"How many times has his father reached out?"

"Mew-Mew writes once a week," he confessed. "The letters started after Stavros met you in person."

No wonder Asa exited the conversation without another word.

We were going to talk about this. Oh, yes. As soon as he got his head on straight.

The childlike fear of Stavros abducting his mother again had lived in Asa all his life. In his mind, it had finally come to terrifying fruition. Worse, she went missing *after* he had denied and then ignored his father. Repeatedly. As if a single thing he said or did would make a dent in Stavros's sense of entitlement to possess any woman he wanted through any means necessary. But I knew Asa.

He would consider the abduction as retribution for those slights.

He would take responsibility for the crime against his mother. View it as failure to protect those he loved from harm. And then he would stew in his guilt, marinate in his shame, simmer in his turmoil —add crisis idiom here—alone.

As someone who often blamed themselves for every bad thing that happened, I could sympathize.

That didn't mean I would let him get away with it.

CHAPTER TWO

*A*sa hadn't wandered far, and I didn't have to search hard to locate him. The bright, coppery tang of hot blood and the brutal pounding of a heartbeat I knew as well as my own led me straight to him.

Thwack.

Thwack.

Thwack.

I traced the outline of the dowel in my pant leg and sent up a silent prayer I got him to see reason without having to zap it into him. Common sense dictated you avoided spelling loved ones with an untested wand.

Thwack.

Thwack.

Thwack.

"Asa."

The glamour he wore every single day of his life, to make himself less, to make himself more palatable, hung off him in tatters.

Wicked fangs dented his bottom lip as he sucked in sharp breaths between his teeth. Thick horns gleamed high on his head, and his long black hair hung free to his waist.

He was beautiful.

So, so beautiful.

And he hurt loud enough I heard his pain as if he were roaring with it rather than swallowing it down.

"I screwed up." I froze when my assessment reached the bloody pulp left of his knuckles. "I should have thought to protect your family as well as mine."

The tree he'd chosen as a punching bag had lost its outer layer of bark, and its raw flesh was painted crimson from Asa's brutal strikes.

A long, long time later, he found his voice. "No one can plan for every contingency."

"You warned me." I took a careful step closer. "Repeatedly." I saw exposed bone and swallowed hard. "You cautioned Stavros would take no for an answer right up until he didn't, and I didn't listen."

Had Stavros done this? Most likely. But I kept any doubts to myself.

Asa wasn't listening to anything except the voice in his head taunting him, blaming him.

"No." Crimson dripped onto the leaves beneath him. "You're not responsible for my father's actions."

"If I had thought about your weak spots instead of focusing on my own, we wouldn't be having this conversation." A stab of genuine guilt told me that much of my speech rang true. "It was foolish of me to believe I could keep blowing off Stavros without repercussions."

"Rue." His haunted gaze rose to mine. "This isn't your fault."

Slowly, worried he might turn his back on me again, I approached him. "Then it isn't yours either."

He flung the punch so fast, with so much hatred, I didn't see him move.

Thwack.

The tree shuddered, bark sprinkled onto the dirt, and leaves rained down on us.

"Please stop beating up the tree." I gave up on the gentle approach and prepared to get physical. "It doesn't deserve this any more than you do."

"Father took her." As his chin dipped, dark hair curtained his face. *"Again."*

"First of all—" I gathered his ruined hands in mine, "—we don't know that for certain."

More than likely, yes, he was responsible. But we had plenty of enemies to choose from these days.

"Yes," he growled, "I do."

"Secondly, if he is behind this, he's still responsible for his own actions."

"He wants you, I won't let him have you, so he took her. To punish me."

That was Stavros logic in a nutshell, yes. No argument here.

"I hate to break it to you, handsome." I cradled his flushed cheek in one palm and fed a different magic into him. The equivalent of a cup of lavender and chamomile tea, with hints of catnip and peppermint. "I'm not yours to give. Just as she was *never* his to take."

"You don't understand." He crushed his eyes closed. "The other fae never let me forget what I cost her."

"The other fae should have been punched in the face every time they vented their disgust for your father at a boy who had nothing whatsoever to do with his conception." A thread of anger wove through me. "Your mother made a hard choice when she kept you, but she chose you. She wanted some good to come from what happened to her. The others should have lifted her up, not torn you down."

"Weeds thrive where they're least wanted."

"I don't follow." Unable to let him suffer when I could help, I focused on his wounds, forcing magic through him to mend the damage. "Are you calling yourself a weed?"

"Grandmother used to tell me that," he said softly, the fight draining out of him as the spell took root. "An old proverb about surviving in the face of adversity."

"Then I'm a weed too."

The idea I was a survivor was foreign, and I wasn't sure it was the word I would have chosen.

Had I survived? Yes.

Had fewer people survived me? Also yes.

When he noticed I was reversing his catharsis, he flattened his lips, but I cut off his protest.

"I like your hands." I wiggled my eyebrows. "I have better uses for them than that tree can dream of."

A furrow dug across his brow, leaving three perfect rows of self-loathing. "I could have prevented this."

"As soon as you stick a shiny red bow on my head," I pretended to agree, "he'll release her."

"That's not what I meant." His fingers closed over mine. "I would never—"

"I know." The burden of his origin cast shadows behind his eyes, and it broke my heart to see him so tormented by his past. "Believe me, I know."

He would slit his father's throat and seize his throne while it was still warm to protect me.

"Talk to me about the temple." I jostled him when he let the quiet stretch too long. "How is it different from the court?"

"The temple is Grandmother's domain." He flexed his hands, his knuckles pink from new growth. "Our reception will be less hostile there."

"Less hostile is good."

"I would welcome a challenge right about now."

"I could zap you until you see sense." I would never convince him he wasn't to blame otherwise. "I don't want to, but I will."

"I can always gauge your declarations of love by their promise of violence."

"Yeah, well, I'm still working on the feeling-my-feelings thing. It's gross, to be honest. And confusing. Why so many emotions? Hunger and lust are plenty. Really, they're about the same thing. Just two different shades of need."

"Hunger and lust aren't emotions." He tilted his head to one side. "They're...feelings."

"Hmm." I tilted my head right back. "You *feel* feelings. Doesn't that make them an emotion?"

"No?"

"You don't sound sure."

"I'm so relaxed," he confessed, "I'm considering using that stump as a pillow and taking a long nap."

"Good." I slid my hand in his then led him back to our tiny house. "Shower and then sleep."

The steps were tricky, but I got him inside without him face-planting. I called that a win.

"We need to have a talk..." he yawned, "...about you using magic on me without my permission."

Sure.

We could do that.

After he explained why he was hiding those messages from me.

"How about next time, I use my body on you?" I sat him on the bed, removed his work boots and jeans, and left him in boxers that would be so easy to push down his legs. "You could work out your frustration in a more environmentally friendly way."

"All right." He raked his fingers through my hair. "For the trees."

The temptation to taste him won out, and I tugged his underwear around his ankles.

His grip tightened, close to hurting, and his heart kicked into a higher gear. "Rue..."

I took him in my mouth before he got his feet clear of the fabric, and his rasping groan as I savored his salty skin warmed my lower stomach until I burned for him. His hands explored lower, abandoning my hair, his fingers trembling as he stroked my flushed cheeks with his thumbs in time with my movements.

His orgasm tore a growl from his throat, and when I finally raised my head, he claimed my mouth in a kiss that stung the backs of my eyes with its gentleness. He kicked my pulse into gear with stinging bites that burned down my neck as he traveled south.

Things might have gotten interesting if I hadn't forced myself to feed him just enough magic to make his eyelids too heavy to lift and mind too foggy to protest.

Thanks to me, he was too tired for a shower and still a bloody mess. The sheets might never recover.

Oh well.

He was worth it.

Shoving him flat onto the mattress, I tucked him in then combed my fingers through his hair until he was unconscious and purring. Only then did I slip out the door in search of Clay.

I found him on a bale of hay with a piece of grass twitching between his teeth like an angry cat's tail.

"How bad was it?" He spat green when I got close and clamped a hat on his head to shield himself from the unrelenting sun. "I can smell the blood from here."

"He mistook a tree for a punching bag." I plopped down beside him. "He was busted up by the time I got there, but I healed him and put him to bed before he marched on Hael and got himself crowned king."

There was no doubt in my mind if he got there, and Stavros had taken his mother, Asa would gut him.

"He's hogging all the blame?" He snapped the stem in half. "Refusing to share any with his friends?"

"Pretty much." I leaned my shoulder against his. "He's greedy like that."

"He figures Stavros snatched Callula as leverage in a trade for the new object of his obsession?"

"Yep." I hated to add fuel to the fire, but he had a point. "Odds are good that's exactly it."

The legacy I inherited from Mom had taught me the pitfalls of being a pawn in a much larger game.

Her sole value to the outside world was a result of the worth Dad assigned to her. She was a chink in his impenetrable armor, and his enemies must have rejoiced the day he fell in love with her. The white witch. The weak link. The knife poised above his heart, waiting for a firm thrust to drive it home.

"It's a very Stavros thing to do." He dusted his hands. "Why do you sound hesitant to believe it?"

20

"Me?" I cranked my head around at his casual tone. "Why do *you* sound hesitant to believe it?"

"There's a time difference between our world and theirs." He adjusted the brim of his hat. "Callula's been missing a day? Two days? Long enough for her mother to worry."

The yin-yang of Peleg's appearance and Callula's disappearance couldn't be a coincidence, not with the Hael factor, but I couldn't figure out where or how their timelines intersected. Until Peleg confessed how he got here, I was stumped.

"Long enough for Stavros to send Asa a list of demands."

Yet we hadn't heard a peep.

The farm might not be on his radar, but my home was familiar territory. It made sense he would go there to lure us out. But had he visited while Aedan was there, Aedan would have reported it. Failing that, Colby would have been pinged on her phone with a motion alert and checked the surveillance cameras. Yet neither of those things had occurred.

Either he didn't have Callula, which seemed unlikely, or he was biding his time before making his move.

"Meet with the grandmother. Get her take on things." Clay rested his elbows on his knees. "Keep your mind open to other possibilities. Enough for you *and* Ace. We both know he's locked on his suspect and won't change his trajectory. It's up to you to make sure he aims at the right target."

"Possibly her too," I added, figuring she would also be predisposed to blame Stavros.

Not that I could fault them. He was a repeat offender, and this had his fingerprints all over it.

"We need to start thinking ahead." He wiped sweat out of his eyes. "Stavros can't sit on the throne forever. Ace isn't an option, so how do we remove Stavros without a proxy?"

"We find a proxy." I made it sound easy. "Talk to me about daemon succession laws."

Royal blood, I had. Royal upbringing? Not so much. I had no clue how one became a king or queen.

Aside from murder. A *lot* of murder. A whole, whole lot of murder.

Not only did you have to seize a crown and behead the person wearing it, but you had to cut down their entire bloodline if you intended to hold the throne long enough to establish a new dynasty.

"Crowns are passed through families. Stavros killed his father, mother, and siblings for the throne."

"No convenient aunts, uncles, or cousins waiting in the wings?"

"He's done a decent job of eliminating threats." He squinted at me. "Sure you aren't willing to give up your firstborn? The crown could skip over Ace and land on your kid's head instead."

A kid who, as heir, would fight for his right to live every single day of his life.

Asa wasn't an only child, not really, he was just the only child to live this long.

The rest had died in pursuit of the crown, and Stavros let them. Encouraged them even. He wanted a worthy successor, or so he claimed.

Me?

I bet he let them rise until the shadow they cast over his rule threatened to eclipse him. Then, conveniently, the right challenger cut them down, or a tragic accident befell them.

How Asa survived was part mystery, part miracle.

Blay was a vicious fighter, and a joyous one. But Stavros had filicide down to an art form. Either the fae blood in Asa had given him an edge, or that same dilution of his blood had convinced Stavros he wasn't a threat.

Until he was.

By then it was too late.

Blay was a powerhouse brawler, an undefeated champ, and Stavros had lost his window of opportunity.

"Tempting, but no." I jerked his brim down over his eyes. "Besides, we might not have nine months."

"Now that's confidence." He shoved it up again. "You think Ace's little swimmers work that fast?"

"Knowing my luck?" I snorted at the idea of me as a mother. "Definitely."

The look he slanted toward me promised the beginning of a pep talk on my parenting skills.

Time for evasive maneuvers.

"You're sure Asa doesn't have a secret twin or a doppelganger in an iron mask tucked away in a tower?"

"Alexandre Dumas?" He clarified the author who dreamed up an excellent solution to a thorny problem by switching a cruel king for a kind one. "They're one and the same in that book. The man in the iron mask was the king's twin brother."

See?

I do read more than improbable shifter romances.

Sometimes.

"Oh yeah." I swatted a black fly eager to bite me. "I always forget that."

How, I don't know, when relatives were often the first ones to stab you in the back.

"When Moran returns Peleg to Hael, I'll have her pick up Ace's copy of the bylaws." Clay brightened from our inkling of a plan. Not much kept him down for long. "We can study it, search for loopholes."

"Thanks." I bit the inside of my cheek, wary of the impulse that prompted me to ask a personal question after evading his. "How do you feel about Moran having a son?"

"It's not for me to like or dislike." His good mood plummeted like a rock thrown into a bottomless pond. "She made that clear when I introduced myself to him, and she yanked him back like I was that sewer clown who eats kids."

A pang hit me when I recalled watching that movie with Camber and Arden, but I swallowed my grief. It was my turn to be a supportive friend to Clay, not hog the spotlight. Grief wasn't a contest. There were no winners.

"Give her time," I returned his advice to him. "She must have been scared out of her mind when she found Peleg wandering around without adult supervision."

Pissed at her ex too, if he…

Oh.

Oh.

"Who is Peleg's father?" I shifted to face him. "Are they married or…?"

"Those are very good questions, and they're also none of my business."

"You've never met business you didn't make yours."

As if realizing this, he pursed his lips in consideration. "True."

"You know, you don't have to throw a giant egg hunt to impress her, or her kid."

"Those are side benefits." He rubbed the back of his neck. "This will be Colby's first holiday away from home. I want to make it special."

She and I had celebrated across the country as I bounced from identity to identity, but we hadn't put down roots until Samford.

"I'm a terrible unmother." I rested my forehead against his shoulder. "I hadn't put that together yet."

"You're hurting." He leaned his cheek against the top of my head. "You both are."

"Still, I should check on her." I fiddled with my wand through my jeans. "See how she feels about it."

"Maybe tomorrow?" His deep voice rumbled through my skull. "Let her have today with Peleg."

"Ugh." I thumped my head against him, which was as good as any brick wall. "I forgot about the boy."

Which meant I also forgot my plan to use Colby to get to the bottom of his mysterious appearance.

"Why ugh?" He stopped me before I jarred my brain loose. "Did you see his little horns?"

"He *flirted* with Colby."

"He's eleven."

"She's *ten*." Closer to twenty, sort of, but that was beside the point. "She's a *baby*."

"She didn't have her blanket with her, so I doubt you have to worry about them eloping."

Few material possessions mattered to Colby, but the blanket Asa knit her that repelled bad dreams was top of the list. She never left home without it. She barely took it off, even during the sweltering summer months.

"That's oddly reassuring." I scanned the area but didn't see a soul. "Where did they run off to anyway?"

Now was as good a time as any to hunt them down and set my plan into motion.

"Last time I saw them, Peleg was helping himself to a snack and a bottle of water." He studied me, noting the unconscious curl of my fingers into my palms. "Should I check in with their nannies?"

"No." I pictured Colby's outrage if she overheard him imply they required babysitters. "And don't call them—"

Boom.

A roiling wave of power rippled the earth beneath me, and I toppled off the hay bale.

The rank waft of black magic paired with a sharp ozone scent stung my eyes and made them water.

"I'll find Colby." Panic beating in my chest, I was on my feet in an instant. "You locate Moran."

With a dip of his chin, he loped toward the commotion, calling out to the first responders for directions.

Based on Clay's latest intel, I sprinted toward the barn and the makeshift kitchen.

The kids weren't there.

While combing the nooks and crannies in case tag had turned into hide-and-seek, I dialed her phone, not holding out much hope she would answer. She was cat-sized the last time I saw her, but the weight of her cell would hamper her speed, and she played to win.

"Peleg missing." A centurion rushed me, speaking in coarse English. "Gone play but not turn."

Foreboding trickled through me, and I got a bad feeling about what we would find. "He didn't return?"

"Girl missing also too," he confirmed. "Go together but not turn —*return*."

"Are you one of their guards?"

"Friend." He shook his head. "No English good." He tapped his bottom lip. "She speak to teach me."

"She's helping you with your English." It was a very Colby thing to do. "Help me find her?"

"Yes," he said with the relief of someone exhausted from parsing our conversation.

Others joined us, eager to lend a hand, and our net spread wider as we searched for the kids.

As time slowed to a crawl, grim scenarios crept into my thoughts, each one worse than the last.

What if Peleg had sneaked Colby past the wards? What if Stavros had a portal waiting, ready to snatch her? What if he was dragging her to Hael as we chased our tails? What if she was hurt?

What if...?

What if...?

What if...?

Strangling my terror, I turned my focus inward, groping for the familiar bond.

Nothing.

I was empty, scooped out and hollow where her warmth ought to be, and bile rose in my throat.

"Rue," Clay bellowed across the field. "We found them."

I kept waiting for relief to hit me, but dread mounted as I raced over with no sign of her. "Where?"

"Behind the old potting shed." He pivoted to run back. "We need to hurry."

"Goddess," I breathed as the rotten cordite scent too familiar after New Orleans hit me.

"The kids' nannies were knocked unconscious," he panted, "but they're both breathing."

A pale leg caught my eye, the skin whiter than its earlier gray, and my stomach dropped lower.

"Peleg." I swear my heart quit on me. "No, no, no."

Blood haloed his head, dying his hair a rich crimson, and his stomach gaped in a mass of weeping gore.

Above him, magic shimmered in an iridescent protective bubble, encapsulating him...and Colby.

From what I could tell, she was unharmed, but his blood spattered her white wings and fur.

"Colby." I hit my knees, grasped for her, but the magic rebuffed me with a jolt. "You have to let me in."

As her mouth formed words I couldn't hear, tears slid down her cheeks, turning her face pink.

This close, I could tell the magic was hers—mine—*ours?* But shock had robbed her of control over it.

"It's okay, sweetie." I fisted my hands until they quit trembling. "I'm here, and it's all right."

Cupping my hands above the curved edges of the magic, I shut my eyes and murmured a spell to shatter her ward. The feedback might sting Colby, the stripping of an active casting often did, but I had to get to Peleg before he bled out on us.

As I dug my fingers into the magic and tore an opening, her screams and sobs poured out, and so did my little moth girl in a flurry of panicked wingbeats.

"I didn't mean to..." She hit the side of my neck. "I didn't..." She stuck like glue. "I..."

The teary confession left me cycling through all the potential meanings.

Colby didn't do this. She wouldn't have done it. She *couldn't* have done it.

She...no...it wasn't possible.

"Are you hurt?" I cupped my hand over her back to still her wings. "Is any of the blood yours?"

"N-n-no."

"Good." I could breathe again. "That's very good."

"Come here, Shorty." Clay scooped her against his chest. "Let's hang back and let her work."

Two fingers pressed to the underside of Peleg's jaw confirmed he was alive.

Alive I could work with. Alive meant he might survive this.

The most grievous injury was the one to Peleg's stomach, but the gash on his head might prove fatal. Careful to hide my actions from Colby, I arranged his insides where they belonged and rested my palms over his midsection. Magic warmed my fingers, sizzling against his wet blood as I fed him healing energy.

Flesh knit closed beneath my touch, concealing the worst of the damage, and I shifted higher to cradle his skull between my palms.

"Come on, come on, come on," I chanted under my breath, sealing the wound. "Wake up, kid."

"Cal…" His eyelids twitched as he fought to surface. "Cal…"

"Shh." I kept going, pushing magic into him. "Try not to speak."

A noise caught between a wail and a roar left my ears ringing as Moran struck the ground beside me.

"Peleg." She tucked her wings in tight. "My boy."

Aware how easily it could have been me in her shoes, I didn't nudge her out of my way to give myself more room to work. I let her hold his hand and murmur assurances, freeing me up to focus every drop of magic in me toward anchoring the boy to life.

When his eyelids fluttered, mine did too, sliding closed with the force of a slammed door.

CHAPTER THREE

"*Y*ou didn't need to manufacture an excuse to come to bed with me."

A faint tingle in my hands and chest left me with a static charge sensation. "Hmm?"

"You could have joined me for a nap without first draining yourself to the point of blackout."

Blackout.

That shot me upright, the top of my head clipping Asa's chin. "I did it again?"

"It was more of a faint," Clay said philosophically. "Very Victorian." He sat at the foot of the bed, my legs across his lap to make room for the three of us. "All that was missing was the couch. I'll add one to my online shopping cart in case there's a next time. I'm thinking crushed red velvet for the upholstery."

With both guys in the tiny house, it felt downright claustrophobic. Or maybe that was the panic clawing up the back of my throat.

"You didn't hurt anyone." Asa tucked me against his side. "You exhausted yourself healing Peleg."

"Healing...?" I dared to hope, even knowing it was foolish. "Is he...?"

"Alive but unconscious." Clay rested a hand on my foot and squeezed my toes. "You saved his life, Dollface."

The pulse roaring in my ears dimmed a few decibels. "Colby?"

"She hit snooze as soon as your eyes rolled back." He puffed out his cheeks. "Poor kid was frantic."

As I recalled her admission, a sour tang flooded my mouth. "What did she say to you?"

"That it was her fault." A frown cut his brow. "I figured she felt guilty for coming out without a scratch."

"Think very carefully before you answer." I broke away from Asa to scootch closer to Clay. "Did anyone else hear her?"

"No one was close enough," he decided, aiming his concern at me. "What's the big deal?"

"The first thing she told me after I freed her was she didn't mean to do it." I shared a worried frown with Asa. "Not that it was her fault, like survivor's guilt, but that *she* didn't mean to do it."

Laughter burst from Clay, who grinned like he expected me to chuckle too. "You don't believe that."

"Pontchartrain." Asa put it together first. "You think she had an episode like yours."

"You were defending yourself." Clay slid his gaze toward the door. "Do you think Peleg hurt her?"

Either that, or he frightened her. More like terrified her. The grimoire wouldn't have gotten involved for funsies. I mean, it would have, but I doubt it could have overwhelmed her without a surge of adrenaline to loosen her hold on her power.

Say, if Peleg dared her to race him past the wards and wouldn't take no for an answer.

"Until one of them wakes," I hated to admit it, "we won't know what happened."

Already riled up from the news of Callula's abduction, I was getting ahead of myself. I was blaming Peleg with no facts to back up a gut feeling that might be nothing more than instinct to strike out at anyone or anything that threatened Colby's safety.

The fastest way to make a mistake in any investigation was to form assumptions based on emotion.

And no, I wasn't saying that because feelings still gave me hives on occasion.

"Why enclose him with her if she was the threat?" Asa hit on the element that bothered me most about how we found them. "And if he was the threat, wouldn't she have left him *outside* her ward?"

"Their scents were the only ones in the area." Clay rubbed alongside his nose. "Aside from every other daemon on the farm."

"The good news is the bad news." I kept returning to Colby. "The guilty party is inside the wards."

"The centuria swore a blood oath." Asa was quick to defend his people. "They can't disobey me."

"Do they have wiggle room?" I turned the possibilities over in my head, aware how carefully daemons worded their cunning bargains. "Does *don't hurt Colby* translate to *you don't have to protect her?*"

"I ordered them to keep her safe at any cost." He set his jaw. "There was no room for interpretation."

Asa was their master, his word their law, but he was new to having them underfoot daily.

When High Priestess Naeema cast a binding over the centuria to guarantee their loyalty to her grandson, she ensured any who harmed him would die by their own hand. An effective precaution at the time, but did the punishment extend to Colby and me? Yet another question for the high priestess.

"I'm sorry." I rested my hand on his knee. "I wish there was another way."

Using his hold over the centuria chipped away at something in Asa. It didn't sit right with me either. But Asa regretted it. Bitterly. Every time he stripped someone of their ability to say no, he struggled to meet my eyes for hours after and couldn't stomach being in the same room as Clay, who was also beholden to a master. His leash might stretch longer than most, but the director held the end in an iron fist.

The complicated feelings Clay was developing toward Moran, who was in Asa's thrall, chafed more each time Asa set down another rule. I worried the friction might, one day, rub their friendship raw.

"Colby's magic is connected to you." Asa's voice came out soft. "Can you tell when she draws power?"

Connected as we were, we could each sense when the other was casting through our bond.

"I couldn't feel her." I shivered to recall the chilling emptiness. "When I reached out, there was a void."

"The ward," Clay murmured. "Do you think it severed your connection?"

"Distance gradually thins our bond, but this was…" I pressed my fingertips against my breastbone. "She was gone."

Never had I been walled off from sensing her, not even at Lake Pontchartrain.

A buzz prompted Clay to reach for his phone, and he put it on speaker. "Moran. Hey. How is—?"

"Colby is awake," she reported, her tone firm and cool. Far colder than any she had used with him in my hearing. "Can I tell her to expect you?"

"We'll be right there." He got to his feet. "Five minutes tops."

The call ended with a decisive click that left me certain there was a target on my back, or Colby's.

"She's not blaming Colby, or you." He lifted his hands in a peaceful gesture. "She just wants answers."

"In her place, I would too."

But if I had to choose between sharing a truth that might damn my little moth girl or giving Moran peace of mind, well, it was no choice at all really.

CHAPTER FOUR

To make the most of existing structures on the property, a half barn once used for storing feed had been selected as the lucky recipient of a makeover that would, after extensive renovations, transform it into a clinic. Until then, its decor, if you were feeling generous, leaned more toward bare necessities than modern amenities.

Medical equipment teetered in boxes stacked against the freshly hung drywall. Medicines and other supplies overflowed a rusted cast iron pig trough too heavy to make moving it worthwhile. And instead of clean benches in a waiting room, we had two rows of scavenged hay bales even an armyworm would side-eye.

Daemons healed fast, but we were courting war on two fronts: with Stavros and with the director.

We had to do better. Faster. We had to be realistic in our preparations for the fallout.

To be fair, we hadn't anticipated requiring a medic on duty until the first volleys were fired.

That had been a mistake.

A grave one.

Judging by the serious man dressed in green scrubs, his top bloody, Clay had found an on-call doctor.

As the person bankrolling this venture, Clay would have chosen the best and paid him enough to overlook the cobwebs, dust, and faint scent of manure that pervaded even long-dormant farms.

"This is Doctor Josiah Nadir." Clay, who clasped the man on the shoulder, handled the introduction. "Dr. Nadir, this is Rue Hollis."

Between the house and the barn, we'd lost Asa to an errand, but I was sure he would catch up as soon as he was able.

"Hello, Rue." Dr. Nadir shook hands with me. "I didn't expect you to require my services so soon."

"Neither did I." I didn't have to look far to spot Moran standing in the doorway of her son's room while two nurses ran tests on his still form. "How's he doing?"

"You saved his life." He offered me a brief smile. "Beyond that, we can only wait and see."

As in, I might have saved him today, but he might not survive the night. "Colby?"

"Right this way." He guided me into the room next door, which had been partitioned to make a semiprivate space for two patients. "Her guardian's burns have been treated as well."

"Burns?" I scanned the room, landing on a lean female with bandaged hands. "You're her guardian?"

The nannies, as Clay teased, hadn't earned a second thought from me. In the moment, yes, that oversight was understandable. But I hadn't acknowledged them once since. I wasn't proud of that. They deserved better. From now on, they would get it.

Even if I was too self-involved to consider their welfare, I should have twigged on the fact they were witnesses who might hold the answers we expected to get from the kids.

"I'm Ivana." She hit one knee and pounded a fist over her heart. "It's my pleasure to serve."

"Thank you." I ducked to catch her eye then motioned for her to stand. "For protecting Colby."

"It's my honor." She rose with a faint grimace. "I will remain by her side, if you'll have me."

The offer, which I accepted, was a sign she wasn't afraid of Colby or what she had—*maybe*—done.

"Ivana." The doctor slid his eyes toward the door. "Would you mind stepping outside for a moment?"

Once we were alone, he led me where a folding curtain blocked the bed on the left from view of anyone who stuck their head in. The one on the right was empty, its mattress still encased in barcoded plastic.

A cat-sized lump in the center was the only indication of occupancy, and when I peeled down the papery sheet, I discovered Colby curled into a ball.

"Hey." I stroked her fuzzy back. "How are you feeling?"

"How is Peleg?" Her wings tucked in tighter. "No one will tell me."

"He's not awake yet, Shorty, but he's stable." Clay posted up on the other side of the bed, opposite me. "Do you feel up to talking to us?"

"He saw me change size and asked how small I could get." Her antennae drooped down her back. "So, I showed him hairbow mode."

"It's okay." I jerked my chin, and the doctor left. "You can tell us."

"No matter what you say," Clay promised her, coming to stand beside me, "you aren't in any trouble."

"He caught me," she whispered, haunted. "Between his hands."

A low rage simmered through my veins when I thought of how badly that could have gone. How badly it did go. For him. "Okay."

"He didn't hurt me." The confession trickled out slowly. "I didn't give him the chance." Her breaths quickened. "He trapped me, and I asked him to let me go, but he laughed." She swallowed hard. "It was dark, Rue, so dark, and I wasn't strong enough. I couldn't get free. I tried. I really did." She stared up at me, the ghosts of her past stirring. "*He* had me, and he wouldn't let go, and I couldn't make him."

A leaden weight attached itself to my heart and dragged it down into my churning gut. "*He* is dead."

"The Silver Stag." Clay grasped our meaning, and his jaw turned to granite.

More than any other moment in my past, I wished I could rewind time. I would claw out the Stag's eyes, cut off his tongue, and slice him open neck to navel. I would leave him staked out for wildlife to feed on him the way he fed on those poor fae girls he killed for the magic in their souls.

To wish it never happened was to alter the course of my entire life, my entire person, but I would trade my happiness for hers any day.

"You had a panic attack." I bent to kiss her forehead. "You were triggered, and you defended yourself."

But from a prank gone wrong or an honest attempt to harm her?

That was what we had to figure out. Until then, we had to proceed with caution.

No answers were forthcoming until Peleg woke, and this time, we wouldn't let him dictate his terms.

"How?" The word got caught in her throat. "How did I do that?"

"You didn't." I smoothed her bristling fluff. "The book did."

How else could I explain away a child, a *loinnir*, wielding deadly magic with such precision?

Colby was light and goodness and wonder. Purity. It was why she shined so bright.

Any darkness, cruelty, or violence came from me, from my power, from the relics. Not her. Never her.

"When the book sensed Rue was in danger," Clay reminded her, "it took measures to protect her."

"People died." I hated that we were having this conversation. "I had no choice, but it happened."

"I didn't call on it." Her expression crumpled as her eyes begged us to believe her. "I didn't use my magic either."

She was well within her rights to defend herself against harm, or perceived harm. The magnitude of her response was the issue. It had been an overreaction, one beyond a mistake she could have made on her own. A punishment she never would have meted out against another child even with provocation.

"I know." I wished I could wipe the guilt from her heart. "The book has a mind of its own."

A rustle of fabric announced Asa's arrival, and I didn't have to ask what had kept him.

"I thought you might want this." He covered her with the leafy-green blanket in his arms then placed her phone and laptop at the foot of the bed. "Do you need anything else?"

"No." Snuggling into the material, she uncurled the tiniest bit. "Thank you."

While Clay helped her log in on her computer, eager to distract her with a virtual reality that was often much kinder than ours (unless you were an orc), Asa pulled me aside.

"We need to get you to the temple." Asa made the call without blinking. "Your condition takes priority."

The condition spreading like cancer through my bond, infecting Colby with dark power and knowledge.

And Asa… He was willing to backburner his mother for her. For my little moth girl.

If I didn't already love him, I would have fallen at terminal velocity right then.

"Your grandmother didn't specify that she was willing to help."

"Fae love bargains."

"Your mother for a possible cure?"

"I don't have a better idea."

"Neither do I." I chewed my bottom lip. "But, on the upside, I might have a way to buy me time."

Showing his fae roots, he asked, "What's the cost?"

"Nothing too bad."

"How certain are you it will work?"

That exact question left me no other choice than to accept help from an outside source. I couldn't afford to use my magic on myself. Not if the book held that much sway over me. It could undo what I had done, and I would remain a ticking time bomb. And through me, Colby would suffer the same explosive fate.

"It has to, or we're all in trouble."

He searched my face, the corners of his eyes pinching, as if he wanted to push harder for answers.

"I'll have to go home." I raised my voice to include Clay in the conversation. "The supplies I need are kept under lock and key."

Understanding darkened Asa's eyes, casting them more emerald than peridot. "I'll go with you."

"Shorty and I have more important things to do." Clay spun the laptop toward her. "We have wild dolphins to tame if we want to catch a ride to the hidden grotto at Mad Macaw Island."

"I wish I could stay." I was tempted to crawl in bed and curl up beside her. "Need anything before I go?"

"No." She yawned as a jaunty sea shanty poured from her speakers. "Check on Peleg for me?"

As far as openings went, it was an ideal one to ask if she knew what Peleg had been mumbling about. But cocooned in her blanket, safe from bad dreams, she relaxed into a healing sleep before the game's opening sequence finished loading.

"I will." I tore myself away from her, tapping Clay on the shoulder as I withdrew. "We won't be long."

"Take all the time you need." He made himself comfortable. "I'm not going anywhere."

Tears pricked the backs of my eyes, and I turned away before I broke down in front of him.

A lifetime of feeling nothing hadn't prepared me for feeling *everything*.

If I ever met an emotion in person, I would punch it in its face.

Out in the hall, Moran had cornered the doctor, demanding answers as to why Peleg hadn't woken.

Once I was spotted, she pivoted to face me, her wings vibrating against her spine.

"What happened to my son?" Her usual calm tone teetered on the brink of demand. "Who did this to him?"

Seeing his chance to escape, the doctor murmured vague noises then disappeared toward his office.

"Moran." An edge honed Asa's voice that warned she was close to crossing a line. "Let us handle this."

"Then you know." Her upper lip quivered over her teeth in a sharp threat. "Tell me."

"We'll sit and discuss this once we have all the answers," I promised. "For now, Asa and I need to talk."

A low growl revved up her throat. "Peleg—"

"—is lucky to be alive." I tasted regret in painting myself as the hero when this was, at its core, my fault. "I understand your fear and anger, I do, but you need to trust us."

Rebellion brewed across her features, shocking in its intensity, but that was motherhood for you.

"Of course." She bowed her head, I suspected to hide her expression. "Apologies for my behavior."

As much as I wished I could take her into my confidence, I couldn't do much without causing irreparable harm to Colby's reputation within the community I was trusting to protect her. That meant choosing her over Peleg and dealing with the repercussions.

I had few absolutes in my life, but Colby was one of them. This wasn't her fault, and she wasn't going to pay for it with her safety or happiness if I could help it.

"Stay with your son. Let Tiago oversee patrols until Peleg regains consciousness." It was the best I could offer her, and her second-in-command was more than capable of stepping into her shoes. "We'll brief you once the situation has been contained."

The twitch in her wings finally eased, and she bowed lower before rising and slipping into Peleg's room.

"Ivana." He beckoned Colby's guardian over to us. "Do you have a moment?"

"Sire, forgive me." She hit both knees with a loud crack. "I failed you once, but I will not again."

"You may rise," he told her. "Speak with us."

"Ask me anything." Her palms flattened on the temporary plywood flooring. "I will answer truthfully."

Worried she was seconds away from planking, I tried to get her talking. "What happened out there?"

39

"The children were playing, and Peleg tricked Colby." She kept her head down. "The boy thought it was funny to capture her between his palms, but she was in obvious distress. I ordered him to release her." She dared peek up at me. "The rest was blinding light and piercing screams." She appeared to realize I was the threat when it came to Colby and broke eye contact. "I was unconscious when you arrived, Princess, as was Tiago. I can't say what happened between then and when I woke."

That was a small blessing, even if the bright punch of Colby's magic might give us away in the end.

"Tiago was Peleg's guardian?" I clarified, hating to admit I didn't know. "How is he?"

"Physically, he is unharmed, but he has confined himself to the bunkhouse until Moran decides his punishment."

"Who ordered that?" Asa glowered down at her. "I wasn't aware either of you had been reprimanded."

Odd how Moran hadn't mentioned they were on the outs when I suggested Tiago step into her role.

"He chose it for himself." She defied her fears to lift her gaze to him. "I would have done the same, but I refused to leave my charge."

Ah. That would explain it. Maybe they could talk it out and still get Moran some time off with Peleg.

"You made the right call." I motioned for her to stand. "I appreciate you sticking with Colby, and I expect to find you outside the door when we return."

"Yes, Princess." She rose with a fist over her heart. "I won't leave her side."

As much as I wished she would rest, especially with Clay on duty, she wouldn't budge while convinced she had something to prove to us. The quicker I helped her atone, the quicker she would forgive herself.

"Do you want help with those hands?" I examined the bandages, which were fresh and clean. "I can heal the worst of it, if you let me."

"No." She flexed her mittened fingers. "I deserve a reminder of today."

Keeping my opinion to myself was the best option to avoid

another round of the blame game no one could win. She wanted to suffer. She had been taught brutal punishments were right and good for those of her station. As much as it disturbed me, she found comfort in it, so I wouldn't yank off her security blanket just yet. But slowly, I would peel back the corner until she was ready to kick it off herself.

Neither Asa nor I spoke on the way to the SUV, but when the door shut behind me, he had his argument ready.

"You're going to use an artifact."

"I am." I fastened my seat belt. "One that will dampen my power."

"Are you sure that's wise?"

"I got lucky with the Toussaints." I pulled out my cell and checked for messages. "Next time I might not."

The Toussaints were black witches. Black witches were, by definition, bad people.

Like you used to be? Or like you still are? Can you even tell the difference?

The voice in my head was brutal as it flayed me open, but my past actions had put the knife in its hand.

"We don't need another Peleg." I had to try to fight back, or else my negligence enabled the grimoire. "We can't risk harming innocents."

Not with Colby acting as a conduit for the grimoire's overprotective power surges.

"You're right." He cranked the engine then put the vehicle in drive. "Will this artifact protect Colby?"

"I'm the one wearing the grimoire. Its hooks are in me." I feared they had been sinking in since the first time I brushed my fingers across its cover. It had recognized me long before I identified it. "If I magically neuter myself, she ought to be safe from any spillover."

If Clay were here, he would be quick to ask if I meant *spay* rather than *neuter*, and I would crack a smile. Without him, I couldn't get my lips to move, let alone curve upward at my own joke.

Any block on my powers that required removal before I could use them was a risk in battle. Trust was key for this to be a feasible short-term solution. Until I freed myself, I would be a liability. But it was that, or I had to get better about writing condolence cards.

There were no staggered mountain ranges, vast open oceans, or endless prairies between the farm and my home. Just a stretch of dirt road freckled with potholes. Not even a long one at that.

The reminder of how close I lived to my old life lodged like a festering splinter under my skin.

Everything looked the same as we breezed through Samford, past Hollis Apothecary. Everything smelled the same when I stepped out onto my lawn and breathed in the greenness of grass and wildflowers. The creek in the backyard tinkled over smooth stones, cold and swift. Everything reminded me of how much I had lost.

"Rue?" Aedan, dressed only in boxers, poked his head out the front door. "I wasn't expecting you."

"I need to grab something from my room." I swept into the house. "How are things?"

"Quiet." He pulled on a tee he found draped over a chair at the kitchen table. "Too quiet."

"I'm sorry." I forced my pace to slow. "I wish you could stay with us."

"Someone has to keep tabs on Stavros." He flashed us half a grin. "It's mostly the boredom talking."

Now that he was no longer employed by Hollis Apothecary—neither of us were, really—he was working as a laborer on the farm. I had seen him every day since we returned from New Orleans, without Arden and Camber, but it wasn't the same. Nothing was these days.

"Would you like some iced tea?" He reached for a glass in the cupboard. "I brewed fresh last night."

"Sure." I backed toward my room. "Just give me a minute."

"Cookies?" He held up a plate stacked high with treats covered in plastic wrap. "I baked them with Colby during a video chat. They're chocolate chip, but I got hungry and ate most of the bag before our call." He scrunched up his face. "I warned her there are eggshells in there, but she said it was fine. That they're an excellent source of calcium and half the world is calcium deficient anyway."

Spoken like someone who knew they wouldn't be called upon to eat them, shells and all.

"I would love one." I elbowed Asa, whose mouth had puckered like he swallowed a lemon at the mention of Stavros. "He would too."

"Great." Aedan set them on the table. "I'll grab some plates."

In his rush of excitement over our visit, I saw how wrong I had been to move him into the house alone. How selfish. The property was wired for surveillance, inside and out. There was no reason to exile Aedan when Colby could monitor the property remotely.

The house didn't need us.

But he did.

"Pack a bag." I couldn't take the idea of him bumping around this empty house for another night. "You're coming back with us."

The wards would stave off an attack until reinforcements arrived if Stavros decided to use my home as target practice to get our attention for negotiations.

"How many days?" He must have assumed we were rushing off on a case. "Two? Three?"

"All of them." The smile I couldn't find earlier crooked my lips. "You're moving in with us, coz."

Just as I turned toward my room, a flurry of footsteps rained down the hall, and Aedan wrapped his arms around my middle from behind, lifting me off my feet. "Really?"

"Really." I wiggled until he set me down. "We need to figure out a better water source for you than your stock tank pool, but we'll make it work."

"There's a well near the old house," Asa said thoughtfully. "That guarantees you fresh water."

"I might be able to coax more to the surface." He fell silent at our blank stares. "What?"

That was news to me, but I had seen his sister Delma control water on a smaller scale. "You can do that?"

"Aquatae, remember?" Turquoise skin fanned across his cheeks to drive home the point, then he reapplied his glamour. "I can't work miracles, but I can convince streams and creeks to alter their course.

Small ones." He screwed up his face. "Sometimes." A flush burned his ears. "One time I diverted a tiny creek to make myself a pool I didn't have to share with my siblings. We were living on a lake then. The overflow from my pool rolled down into the lake and, over time, burst a dam that flooded a town ten miles away. I got in *so* much trouble."

"Let's not flood the town." I heard a curious nostalgia in his tone. "How old were you?"

"Six." He ruffled his hair. "I was lucky no one was killed. Everyone got out in time."

That explained why his talent hadn't come up sooner. "Can all Aquatae control water?"

"Most can't do much more than nudge a single drop across a flat surface."

"Your power is rare?" I couldn't help thinking we were lucky he was one of the good guys. "How rare?"

"Father was proud when it manifested, so yes." He lowered his arm. "It's skipped a dozen generations."

More and more, I was glad my Aquatae heritage had no bearing that I could tell on my talents.

"I never use it, so I'm out of practice. I never had proper training anyway. No one was around to teach me." He wiggled his fingers. "Besides, it's as good as leaving fingerprints at a crime scene."

Used to running for his life to keep a step ahead of Delma, he hadn't had any real stability until Samford.

That made two of us. Three, if you counted Colby. As many as five, if you counted our little family unit.

"Colby can hook you up with copies of the land survey from the purchase. You can make water sources a priority. *Your* priority. I want you pulled off labor to focus on this." I didn't want to admit it, but avoiding a truth didn't change it. "We don't know how long we'll be living on the farm." That was doubly true, for a different reason after the Colby incident. "Finding or making a ready source the centuria can use for any future agricultural projects isn't a waste of anyone's time."

"All right." He backed down the hall. "I'll go get my stuff."

Most of his belongings remained at Camp Aedan, down by the creek. He was more comfortable beside a fresh water source, and Colby had tricked out his campsite until I couldn't blame him for preferring it to being indoors. With a bounce in his step, he exited the house to gather more of his things.

"That was kind." Asa kissed my nape then hummed softly. "Or was it self-preservation?"

"If you're implying that I invited him to live with us only to avoid his baking…"

"Making an observation." His words vibrated down my spine. "That's all."

Alone together, Asa and I slipped into my room where I shut the door and activated the ward for silence.

The air smelled stale, which shook me out of my playful mood. I hadn't been gone but four days or so, and most of that time was spent in New Orleans. Just like any other case. Yet there was no sense of welcome. Instead, the house radiated absence. As if I had never lived here. Or never would again.

Further proof I was right to extract Aedan.

Mausoleums were for the dead, not for the living. Even if what had died was only a part of me.

"With no one occupying the house, we'll need to relocate your cache." Asa sat at the foot of my bed, falling into old habits. "Do you have anywhere in mind?"

"No clue." I sank to my knees in front of my closet. "I didn't exactly plan ahead."

"Until you decide, Aedan could stay." He watched me. "He wouldn't mind a few more days."

That was the smart thing to do, but I didn't have it in me.

"Did you see his face?" I opened the doors and examined the safe to be sure no one had discovered it in my absence, but the wards remained unbreached, the illusion protecting it intact. "It would break his heart if we left him after I told him to pack his bags."

Magic rippled across my hand as I accessed the otherworldly collection that should have been destroyed rather than given sanctuary. Too bad I had no idea how. This indestructible hoard had been meant to give me an edge should I ever need one. Now I was more of a warden, standing watch over cursed items too dangerous to return to circulation.

Yet here I was, shopping from the safe, risking that very thing.

"Will it hurt?" Asa must have read my indecision. "Artifacts require sacrifice to activate, don't they?"

"From me or others, yes." I located what appeared to be a simple rope, dingy and frayed with age, and held it up for his inspection. "This one draws from me."

Better me than someone else. The whole point was to avoid casualties, not create more victims.

Asa studied the artifact, muscles ticking along his jaw. "Can you control how much it takes?"

"We're about to find out." I hadn't meant to sound flip. "It won't kill me, but it won't be a party either."

Jokes about taking uncharted risks weren't his favorite. "What does it do?"

"This rope is one of the oldest relics I own." I set it on the floor while I rolled up my pant leg. "A religious order blessed several lengths to restrain paranormals. The idea was the rope would suck the damnation out of them, leaving them open to conversion therapy."

"Beatings, bloodlettings, and other classics?"

Ah, yes.

The good ol' days.

Scared of something? Confused by something? Jealous of something?

Then torture it until you convince others of its evil, enabling them to murder indiscriminately too!

"Whoever 'blessed' the rope was a witch. Probably a white one. Between the purpose of the rope and the blood and misery that fed it, it developed a mind of its own." I twisted it around my finger. "It decided the best way to make a paranormal *normal* was to devour their magic."

"You're not convincing me this is a good idea."

"The alternative is Colby killing the next person who triggers her and living in that dark place in her head for the rest of her life."

This would hurt. Badly. Like having my soul cleaved in two. Being magicless would make me a liability. But it would protect her, and everyone around us, until we severed my link to the grimoire.

"The first time it does more harm than good, I'm removing it."

"Deal." I wrapped it around my ankle, tying it into a knot. "There."

"I don't like this." He slid down beside me. "Using it feels more dangerous than the alternative."

"I have a big, strong dae to protect me." I forced a smile as panic slicked my palms. "I'll be fine."

And I was, until the magic woke with the ferocity of a starved tiger and sank its teeth into me like I was a fresh zebra shank.

CHAPTER FIVE

 The stink of burnt hair singed my nostrils, and I blinked awake to find Asa hovering above me. "Hi."

"Hello." He stroked his thumb down my cheek. "Looks like you'll need to choose a new artifact."

"Hmm?" I gulped down more of the acrid tang in the air and coughed once. "The rope?"

"The grimoire took exception to another object impeding its hold over you." He held up two sooty fingers. "The rope is gone."

That smell. *Phew*. Nothing stank more than burnt hair.

As soon as I thought it, I jerked my arm up, but a smudge encircled my wrist.

"Oh no." I searched the floor around me but found only ash. "Your bracelet."

The delicate braid he wove to signal the start of our courtship was a victim of the blast that engulfed the rope.

"The token has no bearing on our fascination." He took my hand. "It was a symbol of intent. That's all."

He was wrong, that wasn't all, but I wasn't sure how to put into words what it had meant to me.

Sure, I had been allergic to its implications at the start. And yes, I had resorted to using an itch cream for it when therapy would have been a more successful treatment for my outbreak of relationshipitis. But it had grown on me.

I liked carrying a tangible reminder of what I was to him, of who he was to me. I wasn't ready to give up a piece of our history. I could kick myself for ruining it, but there was no use crying over immolated hair.

"Rue." He gentled his voice. "I can make you another one."

I didn't want a new one. I wanted *that* one. I wanted mine.

Goddess bless, how childish I sounded in my own head.

Petulant or not, that didn't make it any less true.

"No. It's fine. You don't have to." I rubbed grit between my fingertips. "I just didn't realize how much it meant to me until it was gone."

No surprise there. Life got its jollies sneaking up and dumping *ah-ha* moments on us too late to do anything about them but regret not figuring things out quicker.

Thanks a lot, life.

"The grimoire has proven it will fight your attempts to stifle it." He gave the safe and the treasure within a pointed look. "Will you chance another artifact?"

Without magic, the grimoire had zero control over me. Based on its decisive attack on the rope, I concluded the book was looking out for itself by keeping that link alive and flowing through me.

That…was not good.

In the way Cat 5 hurricanes and F4 tornadoes weren't good.

The contents of my safe tallied in my head, and I was tempted, so tempted, to let the book destroy them all. But the risk of it deciding items without offensive magic might serve a better purpose melded with it, *and* the pendant *and* the choker, was too dangerous. It could absorb as well as destroy, and its discretion cost people their lives. To prevent making an even bigger mess of things, I shut and locked the safe.

"How can I?" I reset the wards then double-checked them. "The risk outweighs any potential reward."

"I agree." He offered me his hand and pulled me onto my feet. "Do you need anything else?"

"A time machine would be nice." I walked into his arms and leaned my cheek against his chest. "Turn the dial back a week ago, and we could have avoided all this."

"Not forever." His lips brushed my temple. "The grimoire was always going to show its hand eventually."

"Too bad it holds a royal flush."

CHAPTER SIX

A blanket of silence had settled over the farm while we were away, and I couldn't help but be reminded of the phrase *the calm before the storm*. I couldn't blame the centuria for the questioning glances they cast at us. Peleg—their commander's son—had been attacked, nearly killed, and they deserved answers.

As much as I didn't want to fret over them turning into a mob and raising pitchforks against Colby, I was a witch. I understood how fear caused otherwise decent and rational people to spiral into mindless rage and violence.

Ivana greeted us outside the door to Colby's room and reported that, aside from a few centurions who came to check on her, each okayed by Clay, there had been no activity since we left. That was welcome news.

Peleg had opened his eyes while we were gone, a good sign, but his consciousness didn't last for long.

His father had yet to show his face, but a reckoning was coming. Even if it was taking its sweet time getting here.

"Hey." Clay stood when we entered the room. "Did you get what you needed?"

"The idea I had was a bust." I glossed over the details, seeing as how he didn't know about the safe or the arsenal in my possession. "I'll have to come up with a new one."

"Bummer." His gaze slid past my shoulder. "What are you doing here?"

"Don't sound so happy to see me." Aedan sidled past us. "Hey, Colby." He plopped down next to her. "How are you feeling?"

The lump under the blanket didn't speak, but she did reach a hand toward him for comfort.

"I wasn't expecting you until tomorrow." Clay removed his hat and scratched his scalp, which shone with sweat. "We have that new tin roof to install bright and early. Don't stay out too late."

"I live here now," he announced, earning Colby's full attention. "I can stay up later. Maybe. Depends on Colby." He swung her arm from side to side, and she laughed as each sway went higher. "Are you up to helping me hire a new crew?"

"New crew?" I assumed this was more Mystic Seas drama. "What happened to the old one?"

"The captain fell in love with a mermaid," Clay said, snickering at Aedan, "and the crew mutinied."

I wish I could say this was Aedan's first mutiny, but he was going to break double digits soon.

Last time—maybe it was the time before?—he prevented his crew from spearing a right whale for meat to feed them and blubber to flense for their lamps. That, as you would expect, didn't go over well.

"She was starving," he protested, cheeks bright. "I was feeding her fish, not writing her sonnets."

"That's not what I heard," Clay mumbled out of the side of his mouth.

"I know some people, but it will cost you. You've got a reputation for ditching lucrative quests to explore the sea and free aquatic mounts from their underwater pens." Colby roused herself to turn over and face him. "Or, if you're tired of the mutiny thing, you could join my crew."

The resurgence of her mercenary streak was oddly comforting, and I gave myself permission to believe to the bottom of my black heart that she would be okay.

"You're a terrible captain," she continued, "but an excellent navigator. No one knows the Mystic Seas better than you. Join me, and I'll let you feed all the mermaids you want. I'll even let you free every aquatic mount we capture in raids."

Last I heard, she and Clay were training dolphins to ride to some island that probably hid an exclusive quest. This sounded like a big concession on her part.

"How can I say no to that deal?" He bent to kiss her soft hand. "I'll sell my ship and—"

"No." She jerked upright, the blanket tumbling off her shoulders. "I'm building a fleet."

Not a concession then. A tradeoff. Always hustling, that kid.

"Doesn't a navigator have to be on the ship with their captain?" Aedan considered his options with the seriousness in which she made her offer. "How will that work?"

"You can stay with me, on my ship. I'll promote Ahmed to captain of yours and Shang to his first mate."

Ahmed and Shang were new to her guild, younger kids replacing teens who had aged out and moved on to more adult pursuits. Still gaming, but with a more mature crowd playing rated M editions.

Aedan had this well in hand, so I angled toward the exit to let him do this thing.

"We should check on Moran." I backed away a step. "See if she needs anything."

A troubled line knit Colby's brow, her grip on Aedan tightening, but she nodded we could leave.

Out in the hall, I shut the door and leaned against it, letting my head fall back onto the wood.

"She's going to be okay." Asa came to stand in front of me. "She's a brave girl, and she's strong."

"I wish she didn't have to be." I ignored the sting of tears. "She deserves so much better than this."

Better than me.

"You're the mother she chose." He kissed my forehead, my nose, my chin. "Don't wish that away."

"I wasn't a choice." I had to keep it real. "I was a last resort."

All that remained when I arrived was her soul, twisted into the Silver Stag's signature doe. Only once he was dying, grasping for any lifeline to sustain him, had he spun her into a moth so he could summon her to him. He would have devoured her. Eaten her whole. And she couldn't have done a thing about it.

Except plead with me, another monster, to save her.

Now she was bound to me, our lives braided together, our power a common source.

I would give it up, all of it, if it meant she got to be that little girl again. If she had gotten to go home that night and walk into her mother's arms. If she got to have ten fingers and ten toes. To age. To grow. To *live*.

"Sire."

Asa took his time facing Moran, and he set a comforting hand on the back of my neck. "Yes?"

"I apologize for my earlier outburst." Her gaze touched on me, seeing too much. "To both of you."

"We were just on our way to see you." I forced myself to stand tall. "We heard Peleg woke earlier."

"For a moment." Her pleasure dimmed between breaths. "If his father comes…"

"We won't release Peleg from his physician's care until he's fully healed and well enough to travel," Asa promised her. "Have you heard anything?"

"No." A shadow passed behind her eyes she was quick to blink away. "And I'm glad."

There was history there. Pain. Anger. Fear. A volatile cocktail.

Whatever kept her son with his father, it was clear she hadn't chosen the arrangement.

Yet another reason why he should have been banging on the wards with demands to see his son.

"Colby's asking about Peleg again," I cut in to spare Asa from pointing out no news was rarely good news. "Do you mind if we stop in to see him?"

"No." A battle between mother and soldier warred across her face. "Right this way."

No guard loomed outside Peleg's door, but that wasn't surprising, given Moran hadn't left his side.

She had forgone the privacy screen, which meant we saw Peleg as soon as we crossed the threshold.

A sheet covered him from the chin down, reminding me of a corpse at a morgue. I shivered but forced myself to examine him. I wanted to see for myself the exact nature of his injuries, without adrenaline roaring in my ears, to determine what sort of spell the grimoire had flung at him.

And part of me, I'll admit, and I wasn't even sure it was the black witch part, wanted to look at him and find someone who deserved what he got for making Colby feel small and helpless again.

But he was just a boy.

A gravely wounded child.

Not a monster that would make this easier to bear.

The doctor had done his best, and so had I. I ought to offer a second healing, but I didn't trust the book. I worried it might recognize the taste of him and finish what it started. There were too many unknowns to attempt it while he was so vulnerable.

"He looks good." I bit the inside of my cheek, feeling like an idiot. "Compared to when I last saw him."

Comfort was an alien language I had barely learned to speak to loved ones. This was infinitely harder.

"I'm grateful to you, Princess." Moran stood at the foot of his bed, her body angled between him and us. One of those automatic mom things you do without thought to protect your child when they're vulnerable. "You're the reason he's still breathing."

"I'm glad I could help." Guilt pushed me a step back, away from her bedside vigil. "Asa is leaving soon."

If the blurted announcement I was bailing on the temple visit took him by surprise, he didn't show it.

Until the words tumbled out, I hadn't known for certain I had changed my mind, but it didn't surprise me.

Colby wasn't well enough for travel, and I couldn't leave her behind and just hope for the best.

"We need to gather more information—" he brushed his fingers down the cold metal rail on Peleg's bed, hesitant to touch the boy, given the extent of his injuries, "—if we hope to prevent another attack."

Attack wasn't the most accurate word choice, but it managed what I had yet to accomplish, putting the gleam back in her eyes as she readied for vengeance I didn't have the heart to say she would never reap.

Not when it meant Colby might wind up with a sword aimed between her eyes.

"You're visiting the fae realm?" Her shoulders pushed back. "Do you require an escort?"

"I'm staying with Grandmother, at the temple." He waved a casual hand. "I'll be safe there."

For a long moment, I wasn't sure she agreed with him, which set my nerves further on edge. "Yes, sire."

When her attention drifted back to Peleg and stuck, I slid my fingers into Asa's and led him outside.

"You didn't tell her your mother is missing."

"I didn't tell her about the fae realm either."

"Clay might have mentioned it." I dismissed the possibility as soon as I gave it life. He wasn't a gossip. Okay. He was a terrible gossip. The worst. But only with us. Not with others about us. "The daemons who did the supply drop could have mentioned you received a letter from your grandmother."

"Reported it to her." He slowed then stopped and faced the barn. "That's what you mean."

Until he framed it like that, no, but also maybe yes. "I don't mean to cast doubt on Moran."

Worse was I couldn't tell if it was a legitimate concern or undeserved blame for her boy hurting my girl.

Feelings ought to come with an instruction manual, some way to tell when you were right or wrong to react a certain way.

Until that happened, I was on my own. A terrifying proposition. I wasn't someone who should be left in charge of my emotions. It was like herding cats on a good day. Most days, *feral* cats. Ones I was chasing with shampoo and a garden hose.

"The centuria is used to reporting to Moran. She's overseen their daily life for a long time." I dug my hole deeper. "That's what I meant."

"Rue." He rolled his thumb over my knuckles. "You got me thinking, that's all."

Aware it was indelicate, I still found myself asking, "Who is Peleg's father?"

"One of Father's generals. Dvorak. No one rises in his esteem by not sharing similar outlooks." Asa scanned above our heads, checking we weren't being monitored. "He first saw Moran when she was twelve or thirteen and became infatuated with her. He went to war a few years later, and when he returned with Father's rival's head, Father offered him a boon."

"He chose Moran."

"Yes." He slowed his pace. "He chose her."

"Peleg lives with him. Are they...married? How is she here if he's there?"

"Until recently, the centuria was posted in Hael, remember?"

Meaning, until recently, Peleg had unlimited access to his mother. Her new post on the farm lent weight to the argument he had hunted her down for the simple reason he missed her, but it didn't explain how he found her.

Nine times out of ten, I let paranoia convince me all roads led back to Colby.

To be fair, eight times out of ten, paranoia was right.

Thanks to the grimoire, instead of focusing on that mystery, we got stuck triaging the poor kid.

"Um, yes. There is that." I flushed at the obvious answer. "He let her go?"

"He couldn't stop her. She is sworn into my service." His lips twisted with distaste. "She's as much mine as she is his." He shook his head. "That alone guarantees he'll come for Peleg. For no other reason than to put Moran in her place."

"So..." I rubbed my hands over my face, catching a fresh whiff of burnt hair. "You probably heard me say I wasn't going with you to the temple."

"Not in so many words, but yes."

"As much as I trust Clay, I can't leave Colby while she's fragile. Or while she's a threat."

But with Callula missing, I couldn't hold it against Asa if he decided to divide in order for us to conquer.

"Any hot tips on Moran's baby daddy before you go?"

"The only reason that explains why he has yet to appear is protocol. He requires approval before he strikes, given Moran is in my centuria. If Father is busy with Mother, he won't be taking audiences. Even with friends. That might buy us more time. But, with the realm differential, it likely won't."

"We need to settle this without any *strikes*." I exhaled. "A daemon rumble so close to Samford will bring the director down on my head, and we can't afford to let him discover what we're doing here."

Namely, that we had recruited the centuria to protect Samfordians against Stavros, and him.

Working from home wasn't really a thing for Black Hats. I was shocked the director had let me get away with it this long. Given the scale of the Lake Pontchartrain debacle, and his vested stake in the outcome, I'd expected him to drag me into the office by my ear the next morning and debrief me on Dad.

Dad outing himself in New Orleans left me with no choice but to admit, yes, he was alive. That was as far as I had gotten before hitting the wall of what reaction the director expected from me.

Surprise Dad was alive? Check.

Hurt the director hid him from me? Double check.

Confidence in any and all decisions the director made? *Pfft.* Triple check.

To maintain access to him would require the performance of a lifetime.

With Colby out of commission and conflict on the horizon, I needed a better plan than the neon question mark currently flashing in my brain.

"Clay knows how to reach me if there's an emergency." Asa didn't point out a message would arrive too late for him to help us. "I should be back before there's a need. Two hours round trip ought to do it."

"Two hours?"

"That gives me thirty-six hours, give or take."

"Bring Aedan with you. We can spare him that long." I set my hands on his shoulders. "You're a prince." I cocked an eyebrow. "Surely that entitles you to a personal guard."

"As you wish." A teasing light entered his eyes. "My princess."

"I'm not going to kick you in the junk for two reasons." I tugged on one of his braids. "One, you wisely called me yours. And two, I need that junk for later."

An adorable flush spread across his cheekbones. "I'm happy to be of service."

"Keep that positive attitude, and you'll earn a promotion." Thinking of Aedan and his recent Mystic Seas demotion, I teased, "You could be my first mate."

"I will be." A rumble poured through his chest. "First and last."

"First and last," I agreed, aware no one in this world or any other could replace him in my heart.

CHAPTER SEVEN

*F*unny thing about visiting the temple. It wasn't *in* Faerie. The explanation Asa gave for this was elegant and steeped in religion, but the bottom line was fae were known for their vices: sex, wine, and bargains.

To curtail their natural tendency toward excess, the original high priestess of The Holy Temple of Divine Reflection, his grandmother's predecessor, created a utopian pocket realm adjacent to the fae realm.

Folks *really* loved their pocket realms around here.

The pocket realm concept called to mind a frogspawn. Each tadpole egg was separate but held tight within the same membrane of their mother realm. Fragile. That was the part that always worried me. How easily eggs were broken.

For ease of access, I elected to create a private entrance for Asa to reach the temple rather than have him walk in through the front door. I anchored it in the yard at home, not too far from where I set the portal leading into the arena daemons used for challenges.

The earth here was in tune with me, which made magically expensive spells cost me less to cast.

Plus, we already had enough security issues on the farm without creating another one.

"I'll be back in two hours," he promised. "I'll meet with Grand-mother, search the temple grounds, and return before you get a chance to miss me."

"I miss you already."

"This will be the longest we've been apart in months." He chuckled. "For me, anyway."

"Every minute you're gone will feel like an hour." I walked into his arms and pressed my face into his chest. "Is that better?"

"Much." He forced me to look up at him and brushed his lips over mine. "Be careful."

"I'm sure I don't know what you mean." I fluttered my lashes. "I'll be on the farm, safe behind the wards."

Clay, who should have been in the SUV, choked out a laugh that sounded a lot like coughing *bullshit*.

We ignored him in favor of a lingering goodbye kiss that prompted loud gagging noises behind us.

This time from Aedan.

We ignored those too.

I really should have left Clay at the clinic with Colby to avoid the drama, but he insisted on coming to provide backup for me in case Dvorak or Stavros popped in for a visit after Asa left.

With a tap of my dowel, I activated the portal and watched Asa step through into a sandstone hallway.

Aedan gave me a sideways hug before jogging into another world with a spring in his step.

The ripple of power eddied before I could see more than a woman shriek at their sudden appearance.

Fingers going to my wrist, I traced the spot where my bracelet ought to be and frowned at its absence.

"This is what I'm talking about." Clay slung his arm around my shoulders. "You and me together again."

"We've been together," I pointed out. "For months now."

"But now we're alone. Like the good ol' days. Just think how much fun we're going to have."

"As much fun as you can have in two hours." I shrugged him off me and shoved him toward the SUV. "We need to get back."

"Well, yes, but then—"

"Then I need to fortify the wards, and we need to send the best spy we've got to Hael."

Asa was too close to our new off-the-books case to see clearly, so I would be his eyes.

"That would be Moran or Tiago," he pouted, climbing in and rocking the vehicle. "No way will Moran leave her son. After what happened to Peleg, Tiago would be the better choice for a redemption mission."

"I'm all for boosting morale, but can he handle this?"

"He's not second-in-command for nothing."

"You know the centuria better than I do." I looked long and hard at the spot where Asa had disappeared and then at my home before I put the SUV in drive and left both behind. "I trust your recommendation."

The grumpy golem huffed and folded his arms across his chest, which earned him the laugh he was fishing for.

"Cook me the dinner of my choosing when this is over," he bartered, "and I will forgive you."

With forgiveness that cheap, even if I didn't see why I was getting punished, I caved fast. "Deal."

"Excellent." The bribe did its job, and he shifted gears. "Does Ace know what you're planning?"

"This is his worst nightmare come to life."

"That's a *no*." A glint sparked in his eye. "Maybe this will be fun after all."

"How much do you know about what happened to Callula?"

"The director gave me Ace's file to read before partnering us," he admitted. "I know the official details."

"Good." I chewed my bottom lip. "Then you can give Tiago tips on where he ought to search."

"You don't want to know," he realized a beat later. "You don't want to invade Ace's privacy."

"Correct." I drummed my fingers on the wheel. "I'm happy to let him open up to me on his own."

"I'm so proud." He pinched my cheek. "My little girl is growing into a woman."

For old times' sake, I snapped my head toward him and bit his fingers to prove I was still plenty childish.

"I would like my previous statements stricken from the official record." He shook his hand. "And *ouch*."

A loud *ring-a-ding-ding* from the speakers announced Clay's phone had paired with the SUV.

"Kerr," he answered in his business voice while signaling for me to remain quiet.

"Why hasn't he come?" Moran's voice broke. "Why is he waiting?"

"I don't know yet." He sat back and dug his phone from his pocket. "We'll figure it out, okay?"

"What I said earlier—"

"Water under the bridge." He turned off his Bluetooth. "We can talk after…if you want."

The call ended, his hand fell into his lap, and he smoothed his thumb across the screen.

"Shut up," he grumbled without glancing at me. "Eavesdropper."

"I didn't say anything. Besides, it's your fault you let your phone hook up with any open network."

"There's an insult in there." He let it slide with a grunt that opened a new topic. "Dvorak."

"He should have made a move by now. Generals don't become generals by sitting on their hands."

"There's no world in which Peleg's appearance isn't linked to Callula's disappearance."

"Agree."

Even when you were in fascination with a daemon prince, two reasons to cast an eye toward Hael didn't come along every day.

"Let's pretend Dvorak took Peleg to the palace with him on a bring-your-kid-to-work day or to train him in how to be a future evil overlord. Whatever. Peleg meets Callula, Callula recognizes him as the child of a centuria member—"

"The centuria doesn't leave Hael, and she sure doesn't go there. Would she know them on sight?"

"Who do you think escorted Ace back and forth for visitation when he was a kid?"

"Moran?"

That would explain why he knew this tidbit of history.

"She's loyal to Ace and only him, which made her an ideal go-between."

"What about Dvorak? Had he claimed Moran by then?"

"Yes."

With Dvorak all-in with Moran, I could see how Callula easily made the leap in logic that Peleg was hers.

"Okay, I'm up to speed." I rolled my hand to get back to the point. "You were saying?"

"Callula gives Peleg a message. He sneaks out of Hael, tells Moran, she tells Ace, et voilà! Insta-rescue."

"That's actually not a bad theory." I had to give credit where it was due. "Better than any I've got."

"Two minor flaws." He pinched two fingers together. "He didn't bring a message, and he shouldn't have known where to find Moran."

"Maybe we should talk to her again."

"I don't like where this is going."

"Asa pointed something out earlier." I made the wide turn up the driveway. "Moran is used to living in Hael with free access to her son. Now she's here—a portal away if anything happens. That's assuming Dvorak would bother to tell her. That can't sit well with her." I kept an eye out for any unwelcome guests hidden in the fields or trees. "Something tells me custody battles in Hael are literal."

"You think she told Peleg where to find the farm?"

"All I'm saying is, if I was separated from Colby and going to an undisclosed location for an indeterminate amount of time, I might be tempted to let a few details slip to ensure she could find me if she ever needed me."

Moran couldn't have been thrilled at the idea of leaving Peleg with Dvorak.

And, just maybe, helping create that situation made her a little quicker to cast blame.

DURING THE FIRST HOUR AFTER ASA LEFT, I WALKED THE PROPERTY LINE and reinforced the nascent ward I set prior to the daemons moving in. It hummed along, strong and steady, the infusion of blood from my bare feet helping anchor it. A reminder of what I could accomplish when my magic wasn't held in a chokehold by a wicked grimoire whose idea of a good time was playing duck, duck, *murder* with bystanders.

Exhausted from the blood loss and a heavy magic expenditure, but mostly the sweat-inducing stress that came along with feeling like I was threading my power through the eye of a needle to scrape off any bad intent, I slumped onto a hay bale.

"How did that feel magic-wise?" Clay sat beside me a minute later. "Did you feel mass murdery?"

"As it happens, I did feel murdery, but I don't think the hunk of junk is to blame."

Too bad grimoire assassins weren't a thing. I would *so* hire one. As soon as I got the Maudit off my neck.

"The Hunk." He rubbed his jaw. "I like it." He motioned at my throat with his hand. "Like The Hulk but less trademarked."

"Co-opting." I patted his head. "The Hunk is now mine."

A commotion behind us caught my attention as three daemons hauled boxes of supplies into the clinic.

Moran greeted them at the entryway with pointed instructions on where to put down their burdens.

This was as good an opportunity as any to tick another item off my to-do list.

"Let's take a walk," I called out to her, standing, but I signaled for Clay to stay put. "We need to talk."

A line crimped her mouth, but she nodded once then waited for me to lead.

We got outside golem hearing range before I spoke to prevent nosy eavesdroppers from interfering.

"Peleg never told you, or anyone else, how he got here, correct?"

I started off nice and easy, like slipping into scalding bath water.

"He was distraught when he arrived, so I didn't press."

"That's a big trip for a little kid. Has he ever made it before?"

"A few times."

"With you or his father I assume?"

"Yes."

"Never alone?"

"No."

"Hmm." I gave her space to fill in the blanks, but she kept quiet. "How did he know where to find you?"

"He must have…"

"Overheard you drop the top-secret location of the farm to someone?"

"*No.*" Her knees locked, and she stuttered a step. "I would never—"

"But you would tell him, right? Peleg. He's your kid. You must have been terrified leaving him with Dvorak."

"What you have to understand—"

"—is you put all our lives at risk by trusting an eleven-year-old boy to keep a secret his father would kill for if it meant getting you back or getting back at you?"

"I told him not to come unless he had no other choice."

"You gave a kid who had never been away from his mom a free pass the first time he missed you."

"I made a mistake. I understand that. I should have asked permission. But Peleg is my *son*." She clutched the shirt over her heart. "Punish me. Exile me if you must. I only ask that you allow Peleg to remain until he has recovered."

"No one is punishing or exiling you." As far as I could tell, she was beating herself up plenty. "Okay, that's not my call, but *I* won't punish or exile you."

"You would do the same."

"Yeah. Probably." I put our stroll to a halt. "That's why you'll have to plead your case with Asa when he returns."

To punish her for a crime I would commit in a heartbeat for Colby was hypocritical, especially since I was still irked over Colby's flashback enough to make bad choices.

"I will endeavor to do better going forward."

Which was not a promise of good behavior where her son was concerned, and we both knew it.

"Clay says Tiago is the best spy we've got."

"He is," she agreed without hesitation, even after the morning's events. "You have a mission for him?"

"I do indeed."

"You want Tiago to locate Callula," she surmised. "If she's in Hael."

"*If.*" I thought of Asa searching the temple. "Who, other than Stavros, would target her?"

Trading her for me was simple and straightforward. It made the most sense given the information at our disposal. But why hadn't he sent his demands? Had he decided to keep her? Had she put up too much of a fight? Had they hurt her? Killed her?

One missing child. One kidnapping. Zero ransom demands. The deficit was troubling.

"No one else would dare." Her cheeks turned bone white. "The prince would slaughter them."

A niggling question in the back of my mind had me asking, "How would Stavros take it?"

"Not well," she decided after a brief deliberation. "He still views her as his to do with as he pleases."

And he wondered why he had to kidnap a woman to get one to spend time with him.

"How familiar is Tiago with the layout of the palace?"

"He knows the public parts well, but he's never been invited into the private wings."

"Have Clay brief him on places Stavros is likely to stash her. That ought to cut down his search time."

"Do you have any other orders for me?"

"No." I massaged the tension coiled at the base of my skull. "That's it."

Sliding my eyes closed, I wished for a glass of water and a couple of ibuprofens. Instead of relief, I got an epiphany. One I had to act on fast. Asa would return soon, and he would not approve of it even a little bit.

Which made it an ideal pitch to Clay.

I found my wayward bestie in a narrow stall in the same barn as the clinic. This one had been overhauled too, creating a sterile-ish environment. A neat row of super-thin monitors leaned against one wall, CPUs stacked beside them. Yards of black cord overflowed a plastic tub, and the single outlet meant to run it all looked ready to beg for mercy. A desk, still in the box, and a chair, half assembled, occupied another corner.

Amid the tech store vomit, a golem I had no trouble picturing as a kid in a candy store inventoried his loot.

"What's this?" I invited myself in and checked his hand to see what made him smile. "That a camera?"

"Yup." He flicked open a manual. "We're using the same system you have at your place."

Seeing as how Colby designed it, I wasn't surprised he approved of the choice.

"Save the high mounts." I noticed a pile of cameras yet to be opened. "Colby would love to help."

"Do I look dumb to you?" He narrowed his eyes. "Don't answer that."

Tempted as I was to walk right through that opening, I mimed zipping my lips.

"I'm allowed to assemble furniture. That's it. Colby would break up with me if I started without her." He assessed me with pursed lips. "Then I'd have to promote my second-best friend to fill her spot, and —no offense meant—I'm not sure you're ready for prime time."

Oh, he meant offense.

"Wonder what she would say if I told her you opened a camera box without her?" Leaning my shoulder against the door, I studied my nails. "That you were, in fact, reading the instruction manual with said device in your hot little hands when I walked in?"

"You wouldn't." He shoved it and its paperwork behind his back. "You're not that cruel."

"You can re-box it if you want, but you can't replace the plastic film." I hit him with a hard truth. "Plastic never lies."

"Damn it." He hung his head. "You caught me." He let the contents of his hands fall to the floor. "What do you want in return for your silence?"

"For you to name your water park after me."

"You ask for too much."

"Then I hope you're ready for a new best friend, Best Friend."

"Ugh."

"That's the spirit." I waved him out into the hall. "As your new bestie, I have a bonding exercise for us."

"Oh?" He perked up at the glint in my eye. "Do tell."

"And ruin the surprise?" I led him deeper into the property. "Nah."

The direction of our walk must have registered, and Clay got antsy. "Where are we going?"

"The shop."

More of a shed about to collapse, but it was stocked with every tool you could imagine.

"Have you decided to make a birdhouse as a welcome home gift for Ace?"

"Better." I entered through the warped door on the south end and ducked under the sagging ceiling. "We're going to play a little game I like to call...brute force."

Clay was the strongest person on the farm and the least destructible. A handy combo. It was half of the reason why he got assigned to me back in my wilder days. The other half being the director's absolute control over him.

"I'm intrigued." He stayed outside rather than go around to the shored-up entrance. "What are the rules?"

"You clip, whack, or saw on The Hunk's chain until it snaps, and I'm free."

"Sounds dangerous." He caught the bolt cutters I tossed him. "I'm in."

What was the worst that could happen in thirty minutes?

CHAPTER EIGHT

*P*rior to New Orleans, I wouldn't have resorted to violence to remove The Hunk, but I was itching to get it off me. This wasn't an ideal time to problem solve, nor was it wise to leave the farm. But I would feel like an idiot if bolt cutters saved the day without involving debts or fae high priestesses.

Though I can't say I felt any smarter when the bolt cutters, an ax, a power saw, and a chisel each failed to make a dent.

"Is that a drip torch?" I backed up a step. "Fire that close to my hair seems…"

…like an invitation to join Clay in the Wigs for Life society.

"Cool?" He brandished the tool for prescribed burning. "Neat?"

"Why is it dribbling?"

"Oh, that's the gas and diesel fuel mixture."

"You want to douse me in accelerant, set me on fire, and hope it melts the chain and not my face?"

"Hmm." He considered the steady *drip, drip, drip.* "When you put it like that, it does sound like a bad idea."

Back in the day, I would have leapt at the harebrained scheme, certain I could shield myself or simply eat a heart later to regenerate any flesh I lost. (Though hair was trickier.) But I couldn't trust that kind of magic expenditure with The Hunk already keyed up and fighting for its life.

Any blowback as it protected itself, and me, might send the farm up in flames.

That was why we conducted our experiment five miles away from it, about ten miles from anything else.

That was beyond the known blast radius of my tainted powers, and so far, The Hunk had been downright polite about our attempts to disassemble it. Just as it had spared Blay and Asa on the shores of Lake Pontchartrain, it appeared to have little interest in harming Clay.

Smart of it to realize I would dedicate the rest of my life to destroying it if it harmed a loved one.

And that kind of sentience was exactly why I would have to smite it anyway.

"Not that I'm adverse to embracing a good bad idea," he continued, "but I wasn't actually going to use it on you." He lifted the cannister. "We were looking for this yesterday to create a fire line for aerial drills. We thought a burned grid might be easier for the daemons to see from the air. No chance of it washing away either."

And no one on the ground would suspect it was anything other than a common aspect of country living.

"I leave you two alone for a couple of hours, and this is what I find?"

Asa waded through the thigh-high brush to reach us, exhaustion dogging his steps.

"You're back." I ran at him and flung myself against his chest. "Where's Aedan?"

Impact knocked him down, and he landed on his butt with me straddling his hips.

"Where do you think?" His lips ticked up in a smile. "Off to earn his spot as navigator."

Colby would be thrilled for the company since I had stolen hers. Maybe he could perk her up for a bit.

"On that note—" Clay packed up his toy, "—I'm out."

"Don't you want to know what he learned at the temple?"

"Not as much as I *don't* want to learn how fast you two can get naked." He set out. "Byyye."

"Tiago flew over about five minutes ago." Asa gripped my waist. "That's why he's in a hurry."

Nosy golem wanted to get the news first.

"He's such a turd." I wrapped my arms around Asa's neck. "But he did leave us alone."

"Only because he knows we don't have time to enjoy it." He chuckled against my throat. "Help me up?"

Leaning back, I noticed the dark circles under his eyes and smoothed my thumbs over them.

"Always." I stood and offered him a hand. "Did you sleep at all while you were gone?"

"There was no time." He rose with a stiffness that spoke of sitting for too long. "What were you and Clay doing?"

"Trying mundane ways to get rid of The Hunk."

"The...Hunk?"

"The Hunk." I recalled what Clay said. "Like The Hulk but less trademarked."

"Did you make any progress?" He looked me over top to toe. "More importantly, did you get hurt?"

"No and no." I meshed our fingers and began the walk back, eager to get him safe behind wards again. "Pretty sure it was mocking us. It didn't lash out at Clay once. Just sat there and let us try and fail to our hearts' content."

"Hopefully Grandmother will have more luck."

"How did that go?"

"She's researching a solution for you." His expression grew brittle. "She hopes to have an answer by the time we deliver my mother to the temple."

"Tit for tat," I grumbled at the confirmation we had to give help to receive it.

"I shouldn't have gone. There was nothing to learn. No clues about Mother's disappearance. No quick fix for the choker." He slanted his gaze toward me. "But I appreciate you letting me go."

"I don't *let* you do anything."

"Still, the visit was selfish." He grew pensive. "A little boy's impulse."

Maybe, maybe not.

Our pasts, no matter how much we wished it otherwise, held the power to influence our present.

All I knew for certain was he would never forgive himself if he hadn't gone, if he didn't exhaust every available avenue to locating his mother.

"You mentioned Tiago." I had turned this into a no-fly zone. The others would have intercepted him if he attempted to pass through while Clay and I were busy making poor life choices. "Moran told you about his mission?"

"She did, but I wanted to find you first."

"To borrow my brain or out of fear Clay was about to light me up?"

"Both." His fingers teased under my shirt to rest on bare skin. "How did you two ever get anything done as partners?"

"You'd be surprised how much time you have for pranks and shenanigans when you're single."

"Do you think he misses those days?" He cut me a look that hinted he might not be thinking only of Clay. "Just the two of you?"

To honor the seriousness in which he asked the question, I took my time formulating an answer.

"No." I swatted a fly buzzing my hair. "I was a full-time job. He spent his days and nights keeping me alive and out of as much trouble as he could manage while trying to open my eyes to the world beyond blood and hearts and death and power. To accomplish that, he did a *lot* of very stupid things to distract me from what I craved most back then."

I hadn't realized how fragile his hope for me had been, but he had earned the right to caution where I was concerned ten times over.

"You're a civilizing influence on us." I squeezed his hand. "We're much better behaved with an adult on the team." I held his gaze, making sure he knew I meant every word. "We're much better off with you."

"You realize Clay is older than some dirt." He smiled softly as if he understood the difference between what I said and what I meant. "Does he not qualify?"

"*Mature* is what I meant. Immaturity, in his case, can be eternal."

"Thank you," he said after a while, "for continuing the search here."

"I don't believe help should come with a price when you're family." I cringed when I replayed the words in my head. "Not that I'm saying your grandmother is wrong..."

"I knew what you meant." He brought our joined hands to his lips to kiss my knuckles. "And I agree."

During the walk back, I filled him in on what I had learned, including how Peleg found us.

He wasn't happy but was sympathetic. The best combo Moran could hope for under the circumstances.

The farm came into view, and we stepped through the wards, ready to get some answers.

Tiago, Moran, and Clay waited for us near the tiny houses, and we headed to them.

"Sire." Tiago pounded a fist over his heart. "I bring news from Hael."

The orange spikes usually jutting down his sides had been retracted to allow for his wings.

"That was fast." I rubbed my arms. "How long were you gone?"

"Seven hours."

"Seven?" I did some quick and dirty math then rounded up based on when I estimated him to have left. "Eight hours there is thirty minutes here?"

"It's comparable, yes."

"Did you find Mother?" Asa got straight to the point. "Does my father have her?"

"I heard rumors she was there," he allowed, "but that she isn't any longer."

"Elaborate," he clipped out, patience thinning with his exhaustion. "Tell me everything you learned."

"I will, sire, but first I must tell you." He refused to look at Moran. "I saw Peleg...in Hael."

CHAPTER NINE

"Peleg is here." Moran's wings burst from her spine in a breathtaking spread. "He's in the clinic."

"Perhaps it was a trick, an illusion." Tiago tucked his wings in tighter. "I'm only reporting what I saw."

The hairs on my arms lifted, my nape tingled, and I breathed, "Colby."

The fears from before, that Peleg might be a means to strike at her, snowballed until I was running.

I bowled Ivana over when she stepped forward to greet me, whacked my shoulder in a glancing blow off the doorframe, and scrabbled to the curtain dividing the beds. I yanked it open with one great sweep of my arm, revealing Colby snuggled under the covers. She was out cold, her laptop open and headset on.

A warm hand rubbed circles on my upper back as Asa joined me to stare down at my sleeping moth girl.

"Rue—"

I held a finger to my lips, stole one last glance, then we backed out of the room and shut the door.

While Asa explained the cause for my panicked flight down the aisle to Ivana, and offered my apologies, I located Moran. Like me, she had made a beeline to her child's bedside to check that he was safe. To avoid provoking her already riled maternal instincts, I didn't invite myself into his room. I let her catch sight of me standing in the doorway then motioned her to join us.

"I told you my son was here."

"Yes, you did, but he can't be in two places at once." I sought out Ivana. "Where's Dr. Nadir?"

"Peleg is *here*." Moran flashed her teeth at me, earning a growl from Asa. "My *son* is here."

Between Peleg's critical injuries and Dvorak's looming absence, she was hanging on by a thin thread that Tiago's report of a Peleg doppelganger threatened to cut.

"Then it won't hurt to have his physician verify that."

Too easily, I pictured Peleg as a cute but deadly Trojan horse, and I worried what he might be hiding.

"No one is going to hurt Peleg." Clay rested his hand on her shoulder. "Your son is safe."

"Dr. Nadir is in his office." Ivana pushed her shoulders back. "Shall I fetch him?"

"Yes." I slid my wand into its pocket to force me to think before acting. "Hurry, please."

The four of us kept silent until Dr. Nadir emerged with a thick file tucked under his arm.

"I understand there's some question as to the identity of my patient," he said by way of greeting.

"Information has come to light that suggests it's in our best interest to trust but verify."

Asa took the words right out of my mouth, and I was grateful HIPAA laws didn't apply to daemons.

"Can you tell if he's been glamoured?" I hadn't sensed magic cloaking him, but I didn't know him well enough to be certain of his personal energy signature. "Any chance he's been otherwise augmented?"

"Given the nature of Peleg's injuries, I took X-rays of his skull, hands, and abdomen once his vitals were stable."

Portable X-ray machines cost a small fortune. Clay was really shelling out to ensure the best care to ever come out of a barn.

"Based on his bone morphology," he continued, "I believe the patient is male. Based on the size, and the development of the cranial sutures, he is nine to eleven years old." He lifted the X-ray for us to see. "The elongated canines and horn growth also indicate a juvenile daemon."

"I told you." Moran slumped against Clay as the fight drained out of her. "That's my son."

As much as I wanted to trust that a mother would know, magic was magic for a reason. "And now we know for sure."

Glamours and illusion spells didn't play nice with modern technology, but there were entire paranormal research and development companies whose purpose was to innovate, to provide solutions for how old creatures survived in our ever-changing world. You could never be too careful.

The trusty X-ray machine that pierced glamour today might be tricked with magic tomorrow.

Moran returned to Peleg, done with the conversation, and Clay followed, shutting the door behind him.

"Find someone you trust." I pitched my voice low for Ivana's ears alone. "Post them at Peleg's door. That kid doesn't so much as twitch without me knowing about it. Got it?"

"Yes, Princess." She rocked forward and then settled back on her heels. "Would you like me to go now?"

"Yes." I traded places with her. "I'll stand watch until you return."

With a dip of her chin, she hurried away, and I waved everyone else closer to make casting a privacy spell easier. We needed to have this out, and if Moran couldn't handle it, I would spare her from it.

"How much time have you spent around Peleg?" I checked with Tiago. "I imagine quite a bit."

"I was there when he was born," he confirmed. "I'm an uncle of sorts."

"I hate to keep harping on this, but you're *sure* you saw Peleg?"

Expression tight, he confirmed yet again. "Yes."

Puffing out my cheeks, I palmed my phone and sent a quick text before refocusing on him.

"Peleg is an only child," Asa said, "and neither Dvorak nor Moran have siblings."

"Not a cousin then." I made a fair guess. "Has he sired more children with other women?"

"Dvorak is obsessed with Moran," Tiago said, "to the point of monogamy."

Never quite heard it phrased like that, but okay. "Any idea who the boy could be?"

"You believe me?" His shoulders lowered as if I had set a five-pound weight on each of them. "That I saw him?"

"I believe that you believe you saw him." I thought back on our hot mess of a multi-realm timeline. "I also believe you saw someone meant to resemble Peleg. The question is why?"

"Dvorak wouldn't hide his son's disappearance," Asa murmured. "It's a golden opportunity to thumb his nose at Moran."

And discover where she was living so he could plot how to get her back under said thumb.

"Peleg tried to speak while I was healing him." I watched Tiago for any signs of recognition. "He kept saying Cal over and over. Does that mean anything to you?"

Tiago's forehead did a decent impersonation of an accordion. "Cal?"

"Is anyone on the farm named Cal? Maybe a friend back in Hael?"

"Not so far as I'm aware." His frown deepened. "Are you sure that's what he said?"

"As best I can tell, yes."

"I'm sorry, but I don't know."

"If you think of anything, please let me know."

Asa, who waited for my nod I was done, asked him, "What else did you learn about Mother?"

"A bounty was placed on Lady Callula's head by the high king. The courtiers I overheard were in awe of the sum. They spoke as if it had already been awarded, as if she was in custody." He cleared his throat.

"I paid special attention to the places I was told to search, and I visited the dungeon too. That was where the guards were talking about how she had escaped Stavros not once but twice. How the shame, if word got out, would mean a death sentence for her. And for them."

"Twice as in counting the first time and this time?" I butted in to clarify. "Not twice this time?"

Any escape brought risks, and often injuries, but a second attempt in rapid succession could get her incapacitated to prevent a third. Hard to escape with broken legs. Or arms. Extraction would be more difficult if she couldn't hold her own.

"Then and now, yes." He shifted his weight. "The court believes she is in his possession, but the dungeon is empty, and half the usual guards were absent from their posts. As if they had been given another assignment." Such as seeking a missing prisoner. "I attempted to gain access to the royal wing, but I was recognized in a restricted area and forced to abandon the search." Tiago squared his shoulders. "I could return. Isolate Peleg from Dvorak and question him."

"The palace guards made you." I shook my head. "It's too risky."

"I agree with Rue." Asa put his weight behind my assessment. "A fresh team will handle it from here."

Before I could ask for the roster of this *fresh team*, I recalled Peleg's earlier murmurings. I had meant to ask Moran about it, but she was wound so tight I worried one more twist might make her come undone. If anyone could guess Peleg's message, aside from Moran, Tiago might.

"I have to go there," Asa said under his breath. "I have to be sure."

Cute that he thought I would let him go alone. Adorable, really. There was no chance in Hael of that.

"Where would she go if she escaped the palace? Your estate would be too obvious, and the centuria are no longer in residence to protect her." I cycled through myriad possibilities, but given the number of realms that might be involved, her choices were infinite. "She would have to come to this realm before crossing to the temple or into Faerie, right?"

Neither of them would tolerate a portal into Hael on their lands.

"Dvorak has an estate." Asa shifted gears. "Tiago wouldn't necessarily have to return to the palace."

"With us gone, and Moran distracted, the centuria needs their second in command."

The comment about Moran, which I could have phrased better, earned me a hard look from Tiago.

"Moran's attention is otherwise engaged," he said, smoothing over the tension. "You're right that the centuria needs Tiago to assist her until Peleg has healed from his injuries."

"Where is the kid more likely to be?" I painted apology onto my expression. "The palace or the estate?"

"He trains with the high king's personal guards every day," Tiago told us. "Swordplay, archery, grappling. Sometimes he remains in the palace for other lessons, but often he returns to the estate to meet with his private tutors."

"Thank you, Tiago." I broke the privacy spell to free him. "You can go."

With a respectful nod, he rose. "I will be in the barracks if you need me."

Asa, who knew how my mind worked, was staring a hole through my ear. "What are you thinking?"

There was a whole world of dread squished into those four words.

No sign of Ivana, so I raised the barrier again to give us privacy.

"Okay." I ran through potential scenarios, but I kept hitting a wall. "We haven't eliminated the possibility your mother is hiding out or being held captive in Hael." I tiptoed around my plan. "What you need are daemons who can blend in without being recognized as yours for this mission."

"I don't trust any daemons outside the centuria." He studied me as if he could read my mind and didn't like what was written there. "Certainly not with my mother."

Their affiliation with Asa was well known throughout the kingdom. So was their isolation on Asa's estate. We were counting on those isolationist tendencies to keep other daemons from noticing they had left.

Another centuria sighting, and Asa might as well have trumpeters announce his arrival at the palace.

"Okay." I readied for Asa to go boom. "I propose I take a centurion and target the estate—"

"You want to go to Hael, where my father reigns, who wants you more than any other bright and shiny object at the moment, and sneak around his general's private home?"

"I am neither bright nor shiny nor an object."

"This is no time for joking."

"I'm Deputy Director of the Black Hat Bureau," I reminded him. "I'm an asset. Use me. Let me help you."

"Rue—"

"Don't make me pull rank." I folded my arms over my chest. "I am, quite literally, the boss of you."

We were missing work for this, all three of us, and the director wasn't the forgiving type. He would take our absences out of my hide if we didn't clock in soon *and* with a good excuse. There was even a chance, not that I would spell it out for Asa while he was so stressed, that the director would leverage this against me to claim I was a flight risk. If he got me in the Black Hat compound, he might never let me leave. Everyone looked at me and saw bait for Dad, or Asa.

We didn't have long before I couldn't fix things with the director, and I needed the access to him my position gave me. We needed to make this happen. *Now.* To do that, Asa had to use the resources at his disposal.

"You're right." He raised his hands palms up in defeat. "I hate to admit it, but you're right."

"I know you want to protect me, and I love you for it, but this is what I do." I took his hand. "Think about it. Moran is a goldmine of intel on Dvorak and his estate. I'll be in and out before anyone's the wiser."

"Talk me through your plan." He squeezed my fingers. "You mentioned drafting a centurion?"

"We'll aim for hours when Dvorak is unlikely to be home but when our Peleg imposter might be." Surely someone could calculate a window of opportunity. Otherwise, a guestimate might have to do. "We can tackle that problem while you and your centurion—because no way are you going alone—sneak into the palace and do your best to sort rumors from truths to decide if your mother is there or ever was."

Moran was the natural choice, but under these circumstances, I couldn't help but brand her a liability.

"I reinforced the wards while you were away. Between that and leaving Clay and Aedan, the farm will be secure for a short window of time." I prepared to give myself a headache by using the formula Tiago had given me. "You were gone two hours here, so that's thirty-six hours there."

"It's a sliding scale," he warned, "but yes."

"An hour of real time," I said, deciding that was doable, "would give us eighteen hours in Hael."

Asa didn't protest the number, so that was good. "Who do you have in mind as your escort?"

"I'll need to talk to Moran about that," I said vaguely, but that appeared to satisfy him.

"How do you propose we conceal our identities?"

"How else?" I shot him a cheeky grin. "Glamour."

"We'll need access to the Black Hat database." Asa rubbed his forehead like I had given him a headache. "There are a few soldiers on record with enough rank for their appearance to go unquestioned but not high enough to draw unwanted attention."

That surprised me. "Black Hat tracks daemons?"

"Only those who attempt to assassinate me on the job." His lips twitched. "Those require paperwork."

Black Hat did enjoy putting the *bureaucracy* in *bureau*.

"Hmm." I saw where this was going. "Are we going to resurrect four of the dead ones?"

"That would be easiest," he allowed. "We wouldn't have to worry about bumping into one of them."

"The reappearance of four challengers previously thought dead might raise a few eyebrows."

"Forty-two hours must be my upper limit without sleep." He let his arm fall. "I should have caught that."

The reminder of his sleep deprivation, as well as Ivana's return with her new partner, spurred me into action.

"Go nap." I smoothed flyaways from his face. "Let me handle the rest."

I hadn't lost any time. Or gained it. My body was still on its usual afternoon schedule.

"Wake me when you're ready." He brushed his lips over mine. "Don't let me sleep in."

Under different circumstances, my pride might have been stung when he didn't even try to bargain with me for naked cuddles, but it only confirmed my assessment that he was too tired to set out right away.

As much as I wished for his insight, I had to dig out my work laptop, which was probably in a moving box with a dead battery somewhere, and draft Moran into helping me.

I should have anticipated involving her would end up a two-for-one special.

CHAPTER TEN

One good thing about Clay inviting himself to join in our strategy session was we set up at his tiny house and used his toys. His CPU tower, mechanical keyboard, and vertical mouse flashed in a dizzying rainbow of colors that ought to come with a seizure warning. But maybe that was just me.

"How about this guy?" Clay pulled up our next candidate. "He's missing and presumed dead."

"That's a step above dead-dead," I had to agree, "but what if we scrap the stolen identity idea?"

To go in wearing a dead man's—or presumed dead man's—face invited scrutiny.

What happened to you? Where have you been? Why did you come back, loser?

That last one was the trickiest bit.

If the identity we chose had made it known he intended to challenge Asa, yet showed up alive, he would be heckled for his cowardice. The court would assume he had been hiding and turn on him for their own amusement. Spectacle was not conducive to a stealth mission, so I had to nix that option.

"I'm listening." Clay spun toward Moran and me. "What do you have in mind?"

While he sat in a glowing task chair behind an illuminated desk, she and I shared his twin bed.

"Do you remember when you watched *Death on the Nile* and fell in love with Dame Maggie Smith?"

"Vaguely." He ran a finger around the inside of his T-shirt collar. "Why?"

"You had a program that generated images of your future children."

Back then, the quality was absolute garbage. That was what made it hilarious. But it gave me an idea.

"You must be thinking of someone else." He cleared his throat. "Although I have heard of such things in passing, I have no interest in them myself."

"The idea here is not to get caught," I reasoned. "Why not take two faces from that list, since they're the best comps we've got, and mash them together into a new person? The palace must be full of unfamiliar faces as dignitaries, nobility, and even new recruits filter in and out. No one can know everyone. Dvorak's estate must employ dozens of daemons. Why not play into that? Two new recruits and two new maids."

A knock on the door sent Moran to her feet, and she opened it to reveal her pick for my partner.

"Rue, this is Leandra." Moran rested a hand on the woman's shoulder. "You may speak freely with her."

"It's getting stuffy in here." I rose and crossed to Leandra. "Let's take this to the fire pit."

Gratitude shone in Moran's eyes that I wouldn't delve into her past in Clay's presence.

"So, Leandra, Moran says you're familiar with Dvorak's estate." I indicated a chair, waited for her to sit, then joined her. "Do you think you can help me get in, locate not-Peleg, and get out in one piece?"

"The fortress, yes." She spoke to her hands, which she kept folded in her lap. "I was allowed to stay with Moran when her wounds required attention." Her voice turned whisper soft. "He beat her. Often. She once told me I ought to have my own room. I spent so much time there."

Nothing I said would be adequate, but I tried anyway. "I'm sorry for what you both endured."

"It's all right." She sounded like she almost believed it. "Please, ask your questions."

"How about the grounds?" I leaned forward, elbows on knees. "Do you know your way around them?"

"I'm familiar with the path to the fortress, but Moran forbade me to roam the grounds." She twisted her fingers. "The view from her bedroom includes a grove of citrus trees and a pond Dvorak uses to stable kelpie stallions. There's a kennel too, but I've never seen it."

"Did you have much interaction with him?"

"No." An exhale parted her lips. "He wanted me to understand I wasn't welcome in his home. I think…maybe…he considered me a reminder of what he had done, since that was what brought me there time and time again." She wiped her palms on her pants. "He loves her, very much, and he won't stop until it kills her."

"That's not love," I told her gently. "It's obsession."

"I didn't know there was a difference," she said, brow crinkling, "until I saw you with the prince."

"Yes, well, we'll revisit the topic after the urge to kill anyone who looks at him sideways goes away."

Fascination made me more murdery than usual when it came to him, and that was saying something.

Her soft laughter told me she wasn't taking me seriously, but that was okay.

"You sound like an ideal partner for this mission." I extended my arm. "Will you join me?"

When she glanced up, I expected an expression to match her meek tone, but her eyes blazed with a cold fury. I wondered how often she had kept her head bowed to hide her hatred for Dvorak. How often others, me included, mistook her demeanor for fragileness when she was the kind of strong honed by a hard life. Made tougher by years of forced silence and the inability to advocate for her friend, or herself.

"Yes." She shook my hand. "I would be honored."

"We're aiming for a sixteen-hour window. Pack what you need and wear what you want. No one will see it after I'm through with you."

"You're going to use magic on us." A fragile spark of curiosity lit her features. "Can we be anyone?"

Anyone was a broad categorization. "Who do you have in mind?"

"Giada De Laurentiis."

Idolizing a chef was damning proof Clay was assimilating the daemons to his culture versus society at large. If he wasn't careful, he would have an army of daemon foodies on his hands.

Then again, I could think of worse things to have than a refined palate.

"For this mission," I broke it to her gently, "we're aiming to fly under the radar."

"I understand." She rubbed one of her arms. "It was a silly request."

"Not at all." I smiled to show I meant it. "Magic is very cool, and it can do as many fantastic things as it does terrible ones. You're not wrong to imagine the possibilities. That's what magic is: infinite possibilities."

We sat and hashed out our game plan for a while, but it wasn't long before Clay called to say our new faces were ready. I shot him a quick text with a request for a surprise alteration for Leandra. Then I asked for another favor before we headed that way.

Moran had a hand pressed over her mouth when we stepped inside his house, and her shoulders bounced slowly.

Clay sat with his elbows on his desk, and his head in his hands.

"Do I want to know?" I glanced between them then included Leandra. "Do *we* want to know?"

"He has a file…" tears spilled down Moran's cheeks, "…on his six children with Giada."

"Six?" I bit my lip to hold in my laughter, since I needed his cooperation. "That's…ambitious."

"This is all your fault," he growled at me between his fingers. "Your special request did this."

"Some might say your obsession with Giada did this, but okay. Sure. Blame me."

"Oh," he seethed in my general direction. "I will."

Once Moran had herself under control, the three of us sat on the bed, and he pulled up the first image.

"This will be Ace's cover." He clicked the mouse. "This will be Cho's."

"Cho?"

"His partner."

"Gotcha." I gave them each a quick once-over. "They look dangerous but also bland enough to blend in."

"These mockups are for you and Leandra." He pulled our pictures side by side. "Maids are often multigenerational. It makes sense you two would resemble one another. You could pass for sisters or cousins."

More like the daughters Giada might have with Aedan. The women on screen shared Giada's incredible bone structure, but their wavy hair was the color of sapphires, and their skin the pale blue of Caribbean waters. On second thought, I was ninety percent sure I was looking at exactly that. Baby Aediadas.

Which convinced me Colby's first job when she returned to work should be hacking his computer to see what other mashups lived on his hard drive. In his cloud. Wherever he hid his nightmare fodder.

A delighted gasp parted Leandra's lips, and she rose for a better look at her choices. "Giada."

Despite his sour mood, Clay sweetened toward her. "If Giada was a badass daemoness."

"Giada would be a badass anything," Leandra said with conviction. "Her knifework is..."

Overcome, she couldn't finish her sentence, and I debated if I had made the right call to indulge her.

"If everyone is related to everyone," I ventured, "they'll know we're not who we say we are."

"What if we don't pose as maids?" Leandra picked at her nails. "There's an easier way in."

"Courtesans." Moran caught her meaning and paled. "Leandra, no."

"No one views them as a threat." She forced her hands down by her sides. "They see them as the night's entertainment." She relaxed her fingers from their fists. "They see them as fresh meat."

She wanted us to pose as dinner *and* a show.

Lovely.

"I thought Dvorak was monogamous?"

"Oh," Moran said darkly. "He is."

"The high king sends them as gifts to Dvorak," Leandra explained, "but he passes them on to his men."

"The guards will be cool with that?" I tilted my head. "Us just walking in and doing our own thing?"

"Servants monitor the delivery entrance. That's our way in. They know what happens to the *gifts* sent by the high king. They'll watch until we enter the fortress, but they'll let us pass. They can't imagine anyone lying about what they believe will happen to us, and if we run, worse things than Dvorak will chase us."

Probably whatever he kept in those kennels.

An idea began to form that might give us the best of both worlds. "Do the servants wear uniforms?"

"Yes," they answered in unison, and Moran's expression sharpened in consideration.

"Leandra and I could change outfits after we're in the fortress," I suggested. "Then our similarities would play in our favor. Servants fade into the background. No one looks twice at them except other servants." Leandra's familiarity with the staff might save us. "How likely are they to turn us in if we're discovered?"

"Can you lower my glamour and then reapply it?" Leandra resumed picking her nails. "If there's no other choice? The house staff are mostly females. They know me. They'll cover for us if I say Moran sent us."

"If I use magic, my cover is blown." I rolled the idea around in my head. "But if it comes down to us stripping your glamour, then they'll know I'm not what I appear to be. As long as I don't show my face, we should be good."

Her transparency might save us, but my anonymity, if lost, could damn us.

There was loyalty to Moran, and then there was a reward for trussing me up like a turkey for the high king's delectation.

When you had nothing, not even your freedom, you made survival-based choices. I could respect that. I just couldn't risk someone pinning the red bow on my head I joked to Asa about before turning me over.

"You've got about an hour until full dark in Hael." Clay indicated an app on his computer screen to track the time difference. "I suggest you all be ready by then."

"Do you mind waking Asa in ten?" I lingered near the door. "I can start with Leandra."

A forty-five-minute nap wasn't a lot, especially with Asa's sleep deficit, but it was better than nothing.

"No problem." He waited for Moran and Leandra to file out after me before joining us. "Where should I bring him?"

"Colby's room at the clinic."

"Dollface, are you sure Colby's up to this?" His forehead pleated. "Four glamours is a lot of magic."

"I wouldn't ask that of her." I was surprised he thought I would risk her health. "I need moral support."

Her goodness anchored me, her trust gave me strength, and even without drawing on the familiar bond, I believed her presence would help stabilize my powers.

"Forget I said that." He shook his head. "I know you would never endanger her."

"We're all rattled after what happened." I included Moran in that statement. "I'm jumpy too."

"Do you mind if I walk with you?" Moran fell in with Leandra. "I would like to check on Peleg."

"Not at all." I nodded to Clay. "See you in a few."

Leandra and Moran spent most of the short walk to the clinic in low conversation a step behind me.

Moran had a lot of information to impart and not much time to fill in blanks in Leandra's knowledge.

Before I could horn in on their plans, Clay texted me with my second request, and I smiled wide.

By the time I finished shooting him a quick thanks, I had reached the clinic and Ivana. "Any news?"

Moran drifted away from Leandra to visit her son, and only then did Ivana close the gap between us.

"Peleg was talking in his sleep," she murmured. "He calls out for Cal, but none of us know who that is."

"Not even Moran?" I held my breath until Ivana shook her head, grateful I hadn't had to corner Moran and ask her myself. "Anything else?"

"Not that Perrault heard, no."

Perrault.

I filed away the name as Peleg's new guardian until/unless Tiago got reappointed later.

"Keep me posted, okay?" I spun on my heel in search of Leandra. "Ready?"

Thrusting her shoulders back, she marched toward me, a soldier prepared to go into battle.

That must have been one heck of a pep talk Moran gave her.

"Moran is worried," she confided, which convinced me her orders to speak freely were still in effect.

"About you going back there?"

"Well, yes, but also about the child Tiago saw."

"Do you agree that Dvorak would come for his son if he thought Peleg was missing?"

"If Dvorak believed Peleg was with Moran, yes." Her knuckles whitened as her fingers curled into palms scarred with deep crescent-shaped marks. "It's a perfect opportunity to hurt her, and he never misses a chance."

"Then you agree this doppelganger needs to be identified."

"Yes." She quit fidgeting when she noticed me looking. "I don't trust Dvorak's silence."

That put her in good company.

Waves crashed on the other side of Colby's door, but she didn't call out when I knocked.

Nudging it open a crack, I ducked my head in. "Permission to come aboard?"

Both Colby and Aedan started at the sound of my voice and glanced up from their laptop screens.

Yep.

Just as I thought.

Looting poor orcs and burning their ships. With them still on board. Ships the orcs probably only bought to sail away from Colby's reign of terrestrial terror. Sadly, they were no safer from her on the high seas.

"Rue." Colby beat her wings, dislodging her blanket. "You'll never believe what Aedan found."

"A hidden cove filled with hungry mermaids only he can save?"

Aedan rolled his eyes, aware teasing was my love language. "No."

"A sunken ship with a secret portal to Mad Macaw Island," she trilled. "Can you believe it?"

"Mad Macaw Island doesn't happen to be the name of the next expansion pack, does it?"

Neither she nor Aedan answered me.

Yep.

Just as I thought.

Looting my poor wallet and burning through my savings.

"Hi, Leandra." Aedan offered her a warm smile. "How's it going?"

"It is going," she said haltingly. "I'm accompanying Rue to Hael."

"Hael?" Aedan shot to his feet, and his laptop hit the floor. "That's a bad idea, Rue. A very bad idea."

"Most of mine are," I admitted, ruffling his hair. "I blame it on spending my formative years under Clay's tutelage."

"This is serious." He swatted away my hand. "Does Asa know?"

"I'm going to do you the huge favor of pretending I didn't hear you ask if I need his permission."

Hand covering her heart, Leandra vowed, "I will protect Rue with my life."

Anything he said would make the situation worse, so he bit his tongue.

Smart boy.

"Colby."

Braver than anyone I knew, Colby shut her laptop and crawled to the end of her bed. "I'm ready."

"Hold your horses." I sat beside her. "I have to glamour our team, and I was hoping—"

"I can do it." She puffed up her fur, ready for action. "I got this."

"What I need—" I patted her soft back, "—is for you to be my cheerleader."

"That's it?" Her antennae drooped down her back. "Are you afraid of letting me help?"

"I'm afraid for myself." I saw her hurt melt into understanding and then determination. "Can you keep a baseline on me while I work?"

Any fluctuation in my power, and I had to throw on the brakes or risk the grimoire crashing through me.

"Of course." She climbed onto my lap. "Just say when."

"Leandra." I beckoned her closer. "If you start to tingle, itch, or burn, let me know."

Uncertainty scrawled itself across her features, but she stepped up without hesitation. "All right."

With Colby balanced across my thighs, I took both of Leandra's hands. I focused on the beat of her heart and the thick scar tissue on her palms. I pictured the face Clay designed for her then pulled magic in a slow trickle through my core into my arms and down my fingers before I sent it rippling over her in a thin veil of illusion.

A whiff of rot seeped into the working, and I began to withdraw, afraid to go further.

"You've got this." Colby buried her face in my stomach. "You can do it."

Her confidence allowed me to push through the knot of fear that The Hunk would wrest away my control and sever my connection with the spell. Like scissors snipping a string in two, I cut it free of me and chuckled at Aedan's gobsmacked expression when he got an eyeful of Leandra.

"You've got to be kidding me." Aedan cackled with glee. "Please tell me Clay doesn't know about this."

"He designed it," Leandra told him proudly then blushed prettily. "Do you mind if I find a mirror?"

The simple pleasures of magic were often lost on those who spent it like coins minted in the bank of our heritage. I was born rich, in that sense, and I hadn't checked price tags until I made a go of being a white witch. The cost of that power was more than I was willing to pay now, and thanks to Colby, I didn't have to squint so hard at my receipts. But living on a budget had made me appreciate my natural talent more.

"Go." I shooed her on her way. "You've got about fifteen minutes."

The face would tickle her to no end. The postage-stamp sized outfit...? That remained to be seen.

Sliding her fingers through her sapphire hair, she grinned. "Do you mind if I show my friends?"

"Not at all." I savored the warm spark in my chest. "Have fun with it."

Whatever joy she wrung from the next few minutes had to last her until we returned from Hael.

A bounce in her step, she set out toward the barracks to flash her new look.

"She's cute." Aedan, despite being unhappy about this, couldn't stop smiling. "Her enthusiasm, I mean."

Oh, I knew what he meant. Only one girl was cute in his world. Her name was Arden.

And I wasn't about to bring her up unless he did.

Asa walked in with a vaguely familiar daemon. A male with reddish brown skin and jade hair and eyes.

By now, I had met everyone in the centuria, but I couldn't put names to all the faces yet.

From what Clay said earlier, I figured this was Cho.

"Hey, Cho." Aedan dropped the name, confirming my hunch. "You're Asa's plus one?"

"I am." His grin flashed crimson teeth in a smile he dialed back once turning to me. "Princess, I promise to bring him back in one piece."

"I'll hold you to that."

He laughed.

I didn't.

"We saw Leandra in the hallway." Cho rubbed his throat. "I haven't seen her smile that much in…" He thought about it. "I've never seen her smile like that. You truly gave her a gift."

"She's earning it." I brushed off the praise before it stuck. "You guys ready for your makeovers?"

"I'm ready to get answers." Asa stepped up first. "Have you ever been glamoured, Cho?"

Asa had French braided his hair to avoid *y'nai* interference if someone got handsy with him, and I had an idea how to hide him from them. Might work. Might not. But it was a prime opportunity to test a theory.

And I owed it to Leandra's suggestion we switch our clothes/roles, which I intended to do with magic.

A second illusion would trigger *after* Asa stepped through the portal. That spell would activate a new face Clay created and texted me after we left his house and pair it with the energy signature I borrowed from a randomly selected centurion. The sleight of hand depended on the black nothingness of the portal and the seconds of disorientation afterward to fool the *y'nai* into thinking Asa had given them the slip.

"No." Cho watched me preparing with keen interest. "This will be my first time."

"Ready?" I took Asa's hands. "I've got you queued up next."

"Okay." Colby fluffed her body then settled in. "Let's do this."

The magic came easier for Asa. I knew every curve, ridge, and dip of his body. And I loved him. The Hunk, determined to survive, sensed I had one line no one ever crossed and lived: hurting my family.

As it had when Clay attempted to remove it, The Hunk played very nice with Asa, allowing me to do my best to protect him. So nice was it, in fact, I almost thanked it. A shudder zinged down my spine at the near miss. You did *not* want to thank objects of power. Let alone three of them.

Despite the secondary illusion and its frills, I had Asa ready to go in half the time.

"Nice." Colby fluttered to him and stretched his cheeks. "They should let you design NPCs."

"Yes," I bluffed my best. "I would totally be down for that."

"Nonplayable character," Aedan explained. "They're characters you can't play. That means they can't think for themselves. They perform tasks on a loop and have a set number of actions and responses."

"I know what a PNC is," I lied, and they both pretended to believe me. "Cho, come on down."

Still chuckling, Colby returned to my lap as I took Cho's hands and focused on the image to project.

"Here we go." I breathed out slowly and offered him the same warning I gave Leandra. "If anything tingles, itches, or burns, let me know."

"I'm not worried." He appraised Asa with a critical eye. "Your work speaks for itself."

After casting two complex glamours, my magic was warmed up and humming in my veins. I would have relished the feeling pre-Hunk, but now it made me anxious that summoning too much power or expending too much magic would reveal itself to be the key to unlocking The Hunk's ability to self-govern.

"I'm right here." Colby shrank, flew onto my shoulder, and nuzzled my cheek. "You're doing great."

Once my magic settled, I sent it rippling over Cho to create his disguise.

He snatched his hands back to smack the top of his head as a slender plume of smoke curled above him.

"What's wrong?" I stood in a rush and gripped his shoulders. "How can I help?"

"It's only a little fire." He smoothed his palms over his newly bald pate. "Hair grows back."

Allowing myself to plop down again, I thanked the goddess I had charred his hair and not his brain.

Praised as a miracle hair remover wasn't how I wanted my work speaking for itself.

"Time to go," Clay said from the doorway. "Rue, you're not dressed yet."

"On it." I trusted The Hunk to do one thing, and that was protect its host. "Colby? Do you mind?"

Sailing off my shoulder, she landed on Aedan, and they both watched me transform myself.

"Have you watched *Avatar* recently?" Aedan cocked his head. "There's a certain resemblance..."

Any suspicions I had about the true source material for my blue complexion, I kept to myself.

Maybe the Na'vi vibe to our outfits was a good thing if it kept Aedan from looking too hard at us.

"I'll warm up the SUV." Clay made his escape. "Rendezvous in ten."

"Cho?" I blinked before recognizing him. "Can you locate Leandra and escort her to Clay?"

Halfway out the door, he paused and glanced back. "Does water disrupt glamour?"

Afraid I saw where this was going, I told him the truth. "Magic and water don't play nice, why?"

"Pour dirt over your head," Aedan suggested. "Don't dig for it. Use the sandy top layer."

Dirt was an excellent way to put out fires, if water wasn't an option.

Once he left, I dropped my face into my hands. "That could have gone better."

"It could have gone worse." Asa forced me to look at him. "You did well."

A series of loud honks from the parking lot warned us time was almost up, and we had to get moving.

Either that, or Clay's uncanny sense for ruining any special moment between us was tingling.

Breaking away from Asa, I scooped up Colby for a big hug. "Be good for Aedan and be safe."

"Technically, I'm his captain." She clung to my neck. "I outrank him, so I'll be doing the protecting."

Oh dear.

That sounded a *lot* like the speech I gave Asa earlier.

Maybe Clay wasn't the only bad influence on her.

"Nice try but no cigar." I kissed her cheek then let her flutter to Asa. "Aedan, we'll be back in one hour."

"You be safe too." Aedan snagged my waist and reeled me in for a hug. "When in doubt, bug out."

"Got it." I ruffled his hair again. "Don't fall in love with any mermaids while I'm gone."

"I didn't—" He snapped his mouth shut. "You're an evil woman, coz."

"That's what they tell me." I shoved him back into his chair. "Later, coz."

Hand in hand with Asa, we left the clinic and found Leandra and Cho admiring each other at the SUV.

"One hour." Clay lifted me off my feet in a bear hug. "One minute late, and I'm coming after you."

"Take care of my girl." I wiggled until he set me down. "Take care of you too."

"I know I'm gorgeous—" he struck a bodybuilder's pose, "—but I can fight." He straightened to do some manly hand slappy thing with Asa. "We can hold off a horde for an hour, should the orc scourge attack."

"I'm more worried about Stavros or Dvorak, but good to know about the orcs."

Moran stepped outside the clinic and lifted her hand in a wave Asa and I returned, before going back in.

From my own experiences in parting from Colby when she was hurt, I wondered if she suffered the same fear Peleg might disappear if she took her eyes off him. Until we brought back answers about not-Peleg, I doubted his mother blinked, let alone left his side.

Wishing I had the same luxury, I climbed behind the wheel and drove home.

CHAPTER ELEVEN

*P*ortals worked in a few different ways, but I preferred one of two classic methods.

Anchor one *here* that spat you out at an anchor point *there*.

Or anchor one *here* that let you envision where you wanted to be spat out *there*.

For both the daemon arena and the temple, I used the first method to land travelers in a fixed place.

For Hael, I was choosing door number two so each team ended up at their assigned location.

The small problem with that was both teams had to meet in the middle while I cast a fresh portal spell. It wasn't that big of a deal unless we were, say, running for our lives with my injured MIL slowing us down.

Okay. Enough with the negativity. That would give The Hunk a toehold when I began casting.

Think happy thoughts.

Think happy thoughts.

Think happy thoughts.

To keep my heart light, I focused on a memory of Colby's laughter from the last time Clay challenged her to a dance-off. Even with that held close, I still had to fight the paralyzing fear of what Asa might do to his father if he found Callula in his clutches.

Nope, nope, nope.

Only good vibes.

By some miracle, I stabilized the portal without setting fire to anyone or anything, but it drained me. I had to take care how I spent my magic going forward. The Hunk would seize any moment of weakness to wedge itself deeper, hoping to fuse with me too.

Out of time for more drawn-out goodbyes, Asa brushed his lips over mine before he and Cho left.

"Our turn." I tried to sound upbeat for Leandra. "Got our destination fixed in your mind?"

Fingers lacing and unlacing, she gave me a faint nod that made me worry.

"I release the grip on my magic." I gave her a refresher. "I take your hand, and then we run through."

"Yes. Okay. I'm ready." She shook out her hands. "I know where to go."

As my tie severed with the portal, I rushed to her, linked up, and we leapt through the opening.

Without me feeding it or anchoring it, the portal snapped shut on our heels and knocked us stumbling.

"That was…" I got an eyeful of her chosen drop point. "Are we in the right place?"

When I was a newbie agent, a case brought me to El Yunque National Forest in Puerto Rico. A gargoyle had developed a taste for livestock that grew to encompass small children. As messed up as I was then, I barely recalled the details. Except how I lived on antacids for a month after consuming its sulfuric heart.

Not a meal I would order again.

Gargoyles aside, this lush corner of Hael shared the same tropical rainforest vibe. Had we been in Puerto Rico, I would have thought these oversized trees were rosewood, teak, and mahogany. A few tabonucos, or the next best thing, stood on buttress roots that sprawled under a thin layer of nutrient rich soil as far away as the tree was high. Giant tree ferns created a swaying canopy with delicate fronds, and tiny birds feathered in red, blue, yellow, and green called out to one another in airy voices unlike any I had ever heard.

Asa told me once that the smell of black magic—*my* smell— reminded him of home.

Either he was a polite liar, or he had packed his bags to move into my heart while I was still debating whether to let him leave a tooth-brush in my bathroom for sleepovers.

"The estate is a mile that way." She pointed into the waning sunset. "This is as close as we could get."

"No problem." I checked to make sure she was ready. "The clock starts now."

With a trembling first step, Leandra began our hike. As her confidence grew, so did her stride until I was jogging. I didn't mind the burst of speed. We needed to get in, get out, and get gone before Stavros discovered I was in his domain. I would rather not run into Dvorak either.

We spent our first hour, by my estimation, reaching the front gate. A mile wasn't far, but fallen trees the width of school buses cost us time to scale them, the waist-high root systems tripped us, and the coils of low vines hung like nooses and bristled with thorns, eager to snare the unwary.

On the horizon, a stack of petrified logs came into view, but dark-ness had fallen, and I wasn't sure what I was seeing. More debris? A structure? Then I noted the cold iron gate manned by two beasts with thighs bigger around than Leandra and I smooshed together. I couldn't identify their species, but if I had to name them, it would be *giantae*.

"Keep your head down." She didn't balk, so they must be the usual guards. "Don't make eye contact."

"Got it." I hated lessening my range of vision, but I did as I was told. "Head is in the down position."

Without a hitch in her stride, she sashayed right up to the servant's entrance, exchanged pleasantries in daemonish with the two guards standing there, then strolled in. I swished my hips and followed meekly.

So far, so good.

As we passed under the arch, I saw the petrified logs comprised a perimeter wall. Not the home we had come to search or some other structure. Between us and our target stretched a clover lawn and natural gardens planted with native flora. It was a wild tangle, almost violent in its execution, but beautiful too.

Mind blown.

This was not how I pictured Hael, or Dvorak's estate.

Then again, even monsters grew weary of gazing out onto the landscape of their lives to see only darkness and decay.

As we crested a hill, a menacing fortress carved of black stone was revealed below us.

The transition from oasis to fortress was jarring, like stumbling across a volcano scarring a tropical paradise with its seething magma core.

Two winged guards, muscular but not misshapen by their bulk, posted up at a cold iron door identical to the one set into the outer wall. As instructed, I kept my eyes downcast, but I felt their gazes rake over us as if we were items on a menu they might order from later. The nearest one palmed my butt as I walked past, and he squeezed until it hurt.

The chain around my neck warmed, The Hunk awakening, and it was tempting to just...let go.

"I'll see you later, beautiful." He winked at me. "Perhaps both of you, if I have the energy after my shift."

The urge to draw my wand and stab him in the eye before vaporizing him spasmed in my fingers.

Probably why Leandra tittered behind her hand, looped her arm through mine, and dragged me away.

"We only have so much time before the guards come looking for *the new girls*. Fights often break out for the right to use them first. They will expect us to go to the sauna, bathe, and then dress." She swallowed hard and led me to an alcove where we could regroup. "They'll be waiting for us in the dining hall."

Tick. Tick. Tick.

The clock that appeared in my thoughts warned me they wouldn't wait long, and our time was running out.

"I won't let it come to that." I touched her arm, changing her clothes and then mine. "I promise."

With the ease of long familiarity, she led me through the fortress without setting us in anyone's path.

We crept down narrow servants' passages that ran behind the walls, the paths twisting and turning and climbing until I was dizzy and too confused to ever find my way out again. All the while, I strained to pick up conversations from guests and servants walking the halls outside our corridors, but the stone muffled their words to mumbled nonsense.

"His room is this way." Leandra slid a portrait the height of the wall aside and stepped out. "Hurry."

We scurried to a closet like mice rushing to stuff our cheeks with crumbs from dinner before a cat took notice. She grabbed armfuls of clean bed linens she divided with me, then we strode with purpose to a room at the end of the hall. Swords and daggers in miniature lined its walls, and child-sized armor stood at attention on a faceless mannequin. Small tunics and leather pants spilled over the bed as if Peleg had chosen an outfit to wear to dinner only moments earlier.

Hands fisting in the sheets crushed against her chest, she breathed, "He's not here."

"No." I spotted a plate on a small desk and poked the pastry with a fingertip. "But he was recently."

The treat was missing a bite, exposing a jamlike center, and the flaky crust was spongy, not stale.

"Tiago was right." I dumped the sheets on the bed to free up my hands for snooping. "Someone is living in this room." A basin on a stand used for scrubbing between baths held lukewarm water. "But who?"

Footsteps carried from the hall through the door I left cracked for just that reason.

When a hand twisted the knob, Leandra and I lunged for the ornate duvet and began stripping the bed as if our lives depended on it. Which they might. We hustled through our fake task to avoid drawing undue attention from the young boy with gray skin and white hair who entered the room.

As seen from the edge of my vision, he could have doubled for Peleg.

Only when his easy stride hitched did we curtsey, chins tucked lower than ever, then await his orders.

"You may go." He cut to his window and stared below him. "Return later to finish your chores."

Both of us sneaking glances at the boy, we quickly gathered the linen and prepared to exit.

"What is that...?" He angled his head toward me. "Are you wearing perfume?"

Black magic lingered faintly in my hair and on my clothes, and there wasn't anything I could do about it.

Based on Asa's accounting of Hael, I had expected it to blend in with my surroundings.

"No, sir." I bobbed another, shallower curtsey. "Forgive me if you find my scent displeasing."

With my gaze pinned to the stone floor, I didn't notice his approach until his boots stopped before me.

"Rue?"

A heartbeat passed while I tried and failed to figure out why and how this kid knew who I was by scent.

"You smell of ripe green apples." He filled his lungs. "There are hints of cherry tobacco as well."

As Asa and my fascination progressed, we had begun to carry notes of the other person's scent on us.

But that didn't explain why this boy, who I had never met, linked those smells to me so quickly.

Once my fingers had closed over my wand, I risked lifting my head and still found no answers.

"You're not Peleg." I prepared a spell on the tip of my tongue. "Who does that make you?"

Tears glittered in his eyes and rolled down his round cheeks to drip off his chin. His knees cracked on the tile as his legs crumpled under him. He clamped his hands over his face and sobbed with his entire body, as if his best and only friend in the world had died in his arms and he would never have another.

Leandra, better at reading a room than me, knelt and pulled the child against her side. "Hush now."

"I'm sorry." He sniffled against her shoulder but kept his eyes on me. "I'm just *so* glad to see you."

"Can you help us make sense of what's happening here?"

Magic frothed and foamed across the crown of his head, glimmering as it washed a path down his body. About to jerk Leandra out of harm's way, I glimpsed the person within. Literally. There was a person inside the shell that was Peleg, and I gaped as the rest of the spell slid off her like bubbles in the bath.

"Callula," I breathed, crouching before her to search for wounds. "How...?"

"When Dvorak took me the first time, I wished every single day of my captivity that I could glamour myself into someone else. The maids, the guards, the seamstresses. Anyone. I could picture me walking out the door. I could see me going home." She wiped her eyes with the heels of her palms. "That fantasy kept me alive until I got myself out."

Goddess bless.

Not Cal.

Callula.

Peleg had been trying to tell us where to find her all along.

From the neck of her shirt, she pulled a medallion hanging from a thin metal chain.

A neat crimson thumbprint was visible in its center, and dark fluid sloshed in a channel around the edge.

"You had a charm on when you were taken?"

"I wear this every day. I never take it off. Ever. I even had it spelled to be water repellent."

The fear she must have lived with all these years, that at any time Stavros might decide he wanted Asa to have a sibling or might want to replace Asa outright. She had been terrified enough to have a charm created to enact her fantasized escape scenario should she ever need an out again.

"Peleg agreed to swap." I knuckled my temple as her plan solidified in my mind. "He helped you."

"He saw me chained to the throne after I was delivered to Stavros and recognized me." She wiped an errant tear. "He visited me in the dungeon later and offered to steal a key to get me out, but I had the charm. I explained how it works, and he agreed to switch with me. All I needed was a little of his blood to shape my illusion and grant me access to his surface thoughts to help me pretend to be him."

"How did you fake the training?"

"I didn't." Her chin tipped up the tiniest bit. "I've done all I could do to protect myself, and that included learning how to fight for my life with a sword. I never wanted to depend solely on my will to survive again."

Dang.

Callula was a badass.

The better I got to know her, the more she impressed me.

"I'm guessing he left you with a key, walked out of the palace to hop a portal, and you left for the estate after the guards changed." I had one big problem with their otherwise clever plan. "Why didn't Peleg tell anyone this when he arrived? We wasted so much time. We could have been here days ago."

"His help came at a cost."

"They train them young, huh?" I couldn't be disappointed in Peleg for being what his father had made him, especially when, for a long time, I had been what the director made me. "What were his terms?"

"I got to borrow his life and hide here until Asa came for me. Peleg got to spend six uninterrupted hours with his mother, who he hadn't seen in months, before explaining what we had done."

Except he met Colby, developed a crush, and got sidetracked by puppy love.

"He wanted his fun before she was forced to switch you out."

Their plan might have worked, had he not been unconscious in a clinic bed before his time ran out.

"How did you find me, if he didn't tell you where to look?"

"I sent a spy to listen for rumors of you in the palace, and to get a bead on Dvorak. We had Peleg, but his father never showed to collect. Given his parents' history of animosity, we knew there must be a reason. The spy heard conflicting stories about you, so we couldn't be sure you had been taken by Stavros. But it seemed unlikely you would be anywhere but Hael. Then it became a matter of us finding you. Except our spy saw Peleg with Dvorak. Which was impossible. That was when we knew we had a bigger problem."

And now I knew why Stavros hadn't come knocking on our door.

Callula had given him the slip in a twist worthy of Dumas.

Probably for the best that she skipped the iron mask thing anyway, being fae and all.

"Did you come alone?" She worried her bottom lip between her teeth. "The two of you?"

"Did you think Asa would miss this?" I let myself smile. "He's here too."

Fresh tears sprung to her eyes, and she wiped her face dry with a corner of Leandra's linen. "My boy."

"He would do anything for you." I took her hand and helped her to her feet. "I hope you know that."

"He would do the same for you." Her fingers clenched around mine. "You and I are his vulnerabilities."

"Loving someone should never make them a liability."

"And yet," she said somberly.

"And yet," I agreed with her grim acceptance of the world we lived in.

"We should go," Leandra reported after checking the night sky. "We arrived four hours ago."

As I walked up behind her, I glimpsed a corner of the grove she mentioned, as well as the shore of the pond.

"You're unharmed?" I waited for Callula's nod then asked Leandra, "How far to the rendezvous point?"

Between her and Asa, they had decided where to meet, but I had no good reference for it.

"Two hours." She rubbed her arms at the view. "Maybe three."

"Rendezvous?" Callula worried her charm between her finger and thumb. "Where is Asa?"

"He's at the palace looking for you." A frown slashed my mouth. "He and his centurion will wrap up their search and meet us halfway between here and there. Then I'll anchor a portal, and we'll be home free."

"He'll be fine." She breathed over the medallion almost as if she were in prayer. "He will be fine."

"I'm not leaving without him, and I have no problem killing anyone who takes issue with that."

"We really should go." Leandra touched my arm. "Dinner will commence soon."

"And we're the dessert." I fought off the urge to murder my way through the dining hall. "Got it."

A change of clothes might not be enough to save us if either of the guards from the gate recognized us.

The last thing I wanted was for them to think we were into roleplay.

"Should I reapply my glamour?" Callula glanced between us. "No one questions Peleg's movements."

"If you can, then yes." I opened the door and checked the hall. "We might need you to vouch for us."

The path was clear, but that could change at any moment, and we needed to be gone before then.

After she twisted the charm and spilled fresh blood into the outermost chamber, she spoke a word that I didn't catch and transformed back into the eleven-year-old daemon we had come to find. Her mask rippled into place last, its features nuanced and flawless, and even her voice was a match for the boy I had met.

"Leandra, you're the brains of this operation." I swept my arm like a game show presenter. "Tell Callula the escape plan."

"We sneak into the kitchen." A gentle flush spread over her cheeks at the flattery. "We use the compost chute to reach the bins in the rear garden. From there, we stick to the wall, avoiding the kelpie pond and the grove. Once we're out of sight of the fortress, we locate a hatch near the kennels. It's a maintenance entrance for the aqueduct. We'll have to climb down a ladder about ten feet to reach the tunnel. We'll fit inside with room to spare, but we'll have to crawl against the current. In total darkness. The tunnel leads under the wall and opens into the river about a mile away."

"Rather an aqueduct than a sewer line." Callula frowned. "How do we get past the chef?"

Out of everything Leandra just said, that was what worried her? "The chef?"

"Chef is...territorial." Leandra twisted her fingers into a pretzel. "We're not allowed in the kitchen."

"Maybe not." Sliding my gaze to Callula, I aimed a smile at her. "But I bet Dvorak's son is."

CHAPTER TWELVE

*C*onfirmation the chef despised visitors in his kitchen arrived when Leandra guided us to a silver door crosshatched with deep grooves from, if I had to guess, knives being thrown at it. Weird. Who used precious metal for target practice? Silver was soft, so the door must be an alloy. But what was the point?

"I can smell you," a haughty voice boomed from within. "Why have you trespassed on my domain?"

"I have come with a special request for my father," Callula fibbed with convincing authority.

A gelatinous blob oozed into the doorway, its one giant eye taking us in without blinking.

The creature, whatever it was, had translucent skin the color of peaches, and its dinner was on display in what I wasn't sure you could call a stomach. One adult daemon skeleton floated in its center. Two crows had yet to be digested but were very definitely dead. The same couldn't be said for the lizards swimming through digestive enzymes to battle the elastic membrane holding the chef together.

From what I could tell, there were no definable organs. How did it function without a brain?

Never mind.

I would sleep better not knowing how a giant booger landed a gig swinging a cleaver for a living.

"Your father has had many special requests this week." An appendage stretched from its body, formless and goopy, to jab her in the chest. "Does he not appreciate my menus? Does he find fault with my skill?"

"No," she rushed out. "He is proud to have Buhloe Baruuble as his chef."

"As he should be." The creature, Buhloe, reabsorbed the limb. "What is this latest inconvenience?"

"Might I preview tonight's masterpiece first?" She filled her lungs. "Do I smell skerpikjøt?"

"Yes." A slight widening of his eye betrayed Buhole's pleasure. "I had it brought from the Faroe Islands."

Having raised a son, Callula did a passable impression of a boy eager to be shown wonders.

"You may come." Buhloe made a gurgling noise. "However, your playthings are not welcome."

Peleg was eleven. *Eleven.* The only playthings he ought to have were building blocks.

Leandra lowered her head further, until I was impressed her neck didn't snap, and I tried to follow her example.

The chef made a sticking noise, like chewing gum torn off paper, as he guided Callula to a metal cauldron hung over a roaring fire. The contents of his stomach turned like spokes on a wheel as he wobbled away.

Lucky for us, Callula's leather soles didn't make a sound on the polished stone tiles. That meant Leandra and I could locate the chute without announcing our every step to the chef.

While Callula made conversation with Buhloe, Leandra and I followed Moran's directions to the chute. It didn't take us long to locate, and it was plenty big enough to crawl through. The carrion sweetness of its depths made Leandra swallow convulsively, but it simply reminded me of black magic.

After boosting Leandra into the opening, I caught Callula's eye before hoisting myself in.

Hidden in shadow, I waited to see how she played this, but a soft squeak from behind me shot the gooey eye of Buhloe toward us.

Callula stepped between the blob and the ovens, blocking its view of me, and gestured behind her back for me to go. Forget that. I wasn't leaving without her. Asa would never forgive me. About to jump down and drag her with us, she angled her face toward me and traced a finger from her temple to her jaw.

The message was clear.

Her glamour would be her ticket out.

Turning my back on her left me tasting bile, but her stern expression was very mom-like and unwavering. Until recently, I had no real experience being on the receiving end of such a look, but I heeded her glare.

On hands and knees, I advanced until I glimpsed moonlight reflecting off a bend in the metal chute. Faster and faster I crawled, eager to reunite with Leandra, but I hit a slick patch of foul goop that shot my arms and legs from under me. The slime coating the metal slid me the last yard on my side, and I dropped out of a high gooseneck opening...

...and landed with a squelch and sank up to my elbows and knees in congealed flesh and bone shards.

Corpses.

Dozens of them.

Mostly human. A few daemon. Some fae.

Across the way, Leandra's eyes had doubled in size, and she heaved up her last meal.

No wonder Moran hadn't let her wander. Leandra lacked the constitution for the realities of the estate.

Wading, gliding, almost swimming across the inedible pieces of former entrees, I gripped her hand.

"This is terrible. Horrible. It shouldn't happen. To anyone." I kept my eyes locked on the gooseneck, in case Callula hit a snag in her plans. "We can be traumatized together later, okay? Right now, we have to find Callula and get out of here. There will be plenty of time for therapy after we're home."

I hadn't meant to sound flip, but I could tell I hadn't wholly succeeded in conveying the appropriate level of horror. Hard to fake it when I might not have eaten entire people, but I had consumed my share of their organs.

Footsteps rang on a stone path, and we flattened ourselves among the remains.

"Rue." A head of white hair appeared over the edge of the bin where we crouched. "Are you in there?"

"Yes." Leandra couldn't climb out fast enough, and she didn't look back. "This way."

Our frantic guide cut a path through the garden, under the cover of trees, on her way to the wall.

A long howl raised the hairs along my nape. "What did you say were in those kennels?"

"Garmr," Leandra panted, her voice a shrill whistle through her teeth.

"Garmr?" Callula exchanged a frown with me. "Are those some type of dog?"

"Wait." I grabbed for Leandra, but she slipped from my grip. "The hatch is near the kennels, right?"

Three then four then five more garmr joined in what instinct warned me was a hunting song.

"We're running straight toward them." Callula's pace faltered. "Someone must have reported us."

"The guards." I huffed out a quick breath. "Leandra and I were tonight's entertainment."

Bafflement pinched her features. "Maids?"

"Courtesans."

The pallor that swept through her convinced me death by garmr was a kinder fate than walking into that dining hall.

Ahead of us, coming from the right, I caught my first glimpse of a garmr and cursed under my breath.

The creatures were skin and bone, hairless. Their flesh was black, and their eyes shone like cold moons. I would compare them to a dog, except for their crocodilian heads with punishing jaws and curving teeth.

When Leandra warned me worse things than Dvorak would chase us, she hadn't oversold the danger.

The beasts were cutting off our escape, pinning us between their pack and the fortress at our back.

"The grove." Leandra pumped her legs faster. "Cut through the first row and hit the wall there." Sweat dampened the fabric of her uniform. "Don't slow down, and don't look back."

To climb would expose us, but potential death trumped certain death in my book.

"Do you hear that?" Callula cut in closer to me. "Is that the garmr?"

Wood creaked as we ran beneath the trees, their limbs stretching as if waking from a long nap.

"No such luck." I grimaced at the crackling snap of dry wood. "What are those things?"

Either the pounding heartbeat in Leandra's ears deafened her to my question, or she lacked breath to answer.

Bark sprinkled my hair as the trees ripped their roots from the soil, flinging sap that burned on contact.

What I thought were fruit trees must be the composters for the bin we had crawled out of. Their flowers bloomed white, but ichor stained the petals crimson. Shards of bone protruded from the taut pink fruit like spines on durian. I could only imagine the stench if you sank your teeth into one.

A searing line cut across my ankle as roots tickled over my skin before plunging into my flesh.

A scream lodged in my throat as I gripped a handful of twisting coils and set them on fire.

"*Rue.*"

Blood slicked my leg, but I didn't have time to assess the damage.

Garmr yipped and barked as the scent hit them, close enough for me to make out the froth on their lips.

An entire tree was waddling after Callula, who was strapped down with writhing wooden bands.

"Leandra." I lunged for Callula, hooking my arm through hers. "Wait." I set the knobby roots on fire, and the tree shrieked, an eerie moan raised by the others in the grove. *"Leandra."*

"Now." Leandra glanced over her shoulder, breaking her own rule. "We must climb the wall now."

Unable to catch her, the trees lobbed their unholy fruit, pelting her head, shoulders, and back. The spiny projectiles lodged in her flesh, bursting into pulsating masses that throbbed like broken hearts and bled acid that ate through her clothes down to her skin.

A pitiful cry burbled over her lips, but she didn't slow, and she didn't stop.

Marines in boot camp on Parris Island hit climbing walls with less determination to succeed than Leandra.

Nimble as a monkey, she clambered up and over, leaving Callula and me to limp toward the finish line.

"I'll hold them off." I hoisted her onto the wall. "Try not to let them hit you with that fruit."

Nice sentiment, but she was a sitting duck up there, and we both knew it.

A prickle at my throat warned me the skip of my pulse and tremor in my fingers was rousing The Hunk.

Black magic singed my nose hairs as I reached deep to draw enough magic for a ward.

Snapping my gaze upward, I checked Callula's progress and found her near the top.

Close enough.

The ward would last a few minutes. Maybe. Enough to get me started anyway.

The wood was easier to grip than I dared to hope, gaps in the fossilized bark making tidy handholds.

Fruit splattered to my right as the trees aimed higher, above the ward, and the smoldering juice sprayed me on impact.

No wonder Leandra warned us not to look back. That acid could blind you or burn your face clean off.

Grunting from the effort, I reached the top and swung my leg over, ducking as fruit whistled past my ear. Muscles aching, I made the descent slower, fumbling for handholds as spatter blurred my vision.

I hoped, *really* hoped, Leandra hadn't bolted for the rendezvous point without us.

Callula, at least, would wait for me. Probably. Our split-second of bonding might not have convinced her I was right for her son, but I had saved her life. And frankly, Leandra was in better shape than either of us.

That daemoness could *run.*

Firm hands gripped my hips before I touched the ground and lifted me off the wall.

The bite of the fingers punctured my brief hope Asa had finished up early and come to find us.

"Beloved," Stavros purred from behind me. "I've been expecting you."

Had I masked my scent, I might have fooled him, but my black witch stink led him right to me.

Before I could battle down the warning prickles that threatened to vaporize everyone, cold hands cuffed my wrists behind me. A piece of thin wire slid over my skin and cinched enough to cut off my circulation. My magic thrashed against the barrier, but it was imbued with a nulling spell, and my power couldn't break free.

Not good. Very not good. Extremely not good.

On the edge of my periphery, I counted six daemons with swords aimed at Leandra's frantic heart.

Search as I might, I couldn't find Callula. Too many daemons crowded around us.

No Cho...and no Asa.

I chose to view that as a good thing.

"I hate to disappoint." I couldn't resist provoking him. "Bet you've got plenty of experience in that area."

Claws digging into my shoulders, he spun me to face him then slammed me against the wall and held the blade of a palm-sized dagger at my throat.

"We've already established," I reminded him with a swallow that sliced into my skin, "that you swinging your sword around won't win me over."

"You won't be won," he growled in response, "so you will be taken."

"Do you think you could have taken me fifteen or twenty minutes ago? Before I slid down that chute?"

"And miss the chance to surprise you?" He licked my cheek. "Besides, blood becomes you."

As much as I wanted to smack him, I didn't want Leandra or Callula to pay for it, so I kept calm. Ish.

"Do all high kings lounge beneath walls in the hopes of surprising their ladyloves?"

"Only ones who discover their son sneaking through their palace in search of what he will not find."

A knot formed in my throat I couldn't swallow past, and his answering smile told me he knew it too.

"How did you know where to find me?" I sounded like a bullfrog strangled mid-croak. "Who told you?"

"Do you worry my son gave you up out of fear?" He grinned as if me doubting Asa would please him. "Or is it the centurion you distrust?"

"Neither." I glanced around us. "I figured the *y'nai* tattled on us."

The choker should have protected me, and the extra spell ought to have protected Asa, but...

Lots of *shoulds* and *oughts* in this mission, which probably explained its spectacular failure.

"They have been oddly silent." He took my cue to examine the area. "No." He focused on a point beyond me. "The general is responsible for your apprehension." The skin tightened around his eyes as he said, "I regret to confirm your suspicions, old friend, but it appears your son has betrayed us."

120

A daemon with a broken horn and scarred cheeks gripped Callula by the ruff like an errant puppy.

Chills pebbled my skin as I recognized him from his striking resemblance to Peleg.

Dvorak.

"Where have you hidden Callula, boy?" He shook Peleg. "We know you helped that worthless fae whore escape. You were seen leaving the dungeon moments before she was discovered missing."

Boy? Holy crap. They didn't know.

Vicious determination gleamed in Callula's eyes. "I didn't—"

Dvorak slapped her so hard, her neck popped from the force. "Don't lie to me."

"I don't have her." She spat blood on the dirt. "I left the dungeon alone."

Fae were smooth talkers at the best of times, and they shone at their worst.

What Callula told him was the truth. It just wasn't the answer to the question he was asking.

"Traitor." Dvorak punched her in the gut, and she doubled over. "You will be punished for this."

"He's just a kid." I stepped into Stavros's blade, despite the burn. "You've punished him enough."

A low growl poured out of Dvorak that had magic leaping into my palms and tingling in my fingers.

Fear burned in my chest, slicked my palms, and left me panting for control The Hunk threatened to steal.

"We'll be the judges of that." Stavros snapped his fingers. "Ready the buckets."

Oh crap.

Blame panic, but I had forgotten about the glamour.

Stavros, clearly, had not.

Milky liquid splashed the side of my head, drenching Leandra, and soaking Callula too.

Thank the goddess Callula's glamour was waterproof.

The illusion wrapping Leandra washed down her to puddle at her feet. I could only assume mine had too. It didn't matter, though. Glamour was a tool, not a weapon. It couldn't save Leandra or me now. Besides, the silky fluid dripping down my scalp soothed my enflamed skin better than calamine lotion. A small mercy.

"That's better." Stavros cradled my jaw in his calloused palm. "She's too beautiful to conceal, isn't she, Dvorak?"

"Yes, sire," Dvorak agreed with his mouth while his eyes promised my slow and painful death.

"Excellent." He angled my head this way and that, examining me. "The burns will heal."

A swift stomp to her knee sent Callula crashing onto all fours where Dvorak aimed punishing kicks at her ribs. She curled in on herself, blood and drool sliding down her chin and cheek, but she didn't break. She didn't tell them who she was, which would have both saved and damned her.

"That's enough." I shouldered Stavros and his sticky fingers aside. "Lay off the kid."

Malice in his eyes, Dvorak reared back to kick again, but I dove to cover Callula's head.

His boot slammed into the base of my skull, smearing my vision into a blue-black landscape of pain.

CHAPTER THIRTEEN

*V*oices drifted to me from miles away. Miles and miles and miles. Too far for me to join in.

"Rue is my mate." Asa's voice crackled with violence. "Release her, or you leave me no choice."

No, no, no.

Dreaming.

I was dreaming.

This was all a bad dream.

Please, goddess, let this be a bad dream.

"Are you threatening me, child?" Stavros belted out a laugh. "Am I supposed to be afraid?"

"Release her or find out." A growl poured out of him. "This time, I have something worth fighting for."

I had to distract them. I had to stop this. I refused to lose Asa to a poison throne.

"How did I spawn such a sentimental fool?" Stavros spat at him. "You're a poor excuse for a prince."

Instinct called for my magic to fill my hands, but the void in me howled with the absence of power.

Wire.

I was still wearing the wire on my wrists.

I didn't know if it was a charm or a witch bane or what.

Dull ringing filled my head with white noise that made it hard to think, to plan, and no matter how hard I tried, I couldn't get my mouth to twitch or my eyelids to lift.

The whoosh of flames igniting blew warm air over me, bringing with it the scent of cherry tobacco.

Blay.

As my bruised mind pieced together what Blay was doing, what he was planning, terror dumped enough adrenaline in my veins to burn away the thickest cobwebs sticking my thoughts together. I pried one eye open and parted my lips to scream, *"No."*

Snarling his lip up over his teeth, Blay emerged from the fire of his transformation.

"Blay challenge you." He jabbed a finger into Stavros's chest. "Rue *mine.*"

A dozen or more daemons shifted on my periphery, but none would lift a finger to help their high prince.

"Take it back." I didn't beg, ever, but I was willing to hit my knees for him. *"Please."*

"He hurt Rue." Blay refused to see reason. "Blay won't let him hurt Rue again."

"Please, please, please," I chanted under my breath. "This isn't what you or Asa want."

A gleam of triumph lit Stavros's eyes, confirming the damage was already done.

There was no way to take it back, and I knew it. I *knew.* That didn't stop me from babbling entreaties.

There were too many witnesses. I knew that too. Backing down would make Stavros appear afraid of his son. His pride burned too bright to allow that. Especially after he had been handed a golden opportunity to rid himself of his heir, claim me as his mate, and start the succession line anew.

"Oh," Stavros crooned, "but it's what I want." He snapped his fingers. "Restrain my son."

Dvorak darkened my field of vision, what pathetic amount I had, and gripped Blay by the throat.

Blay let him manhandle him. He even smiled, like he thought it was funny, but Dvorak wasn't laughing. It was almost sad, how the older daemon thought he was going to walk away from this with his heart.

I didn't have to eat it, just rip it out and lob it over the fence to feed his trees.

"Come, beloved," Stavros crooned, helping me sit upright, "and know I earned you fair and square."

Weak as a kitten, I still showed him my claws. "Do you think I'll let you live if you kill him?"

Chuckling, he slid his hands under my back and thighs to lift me. "I'm going to enjoy breaking you."

"You can try." I whipped my head forward, smashing his nose. "Better men than you have failed."

To prevent me from trying again, he fisted my hair and yanked until my scalp threatened to touch my spine. Radiating bolts of agony blasted up my nape through the top of my skull, and spots swam in my vision.

Hello, concussion, my old friend.

A smarter woman would have stopped there, but I had never been in doubt of my intelligence.

Swiping through the air until I located his cheeks, I jammed my thumbs into his eyes.

No.

Wait.

Those were his nostrils.

With a roar, he flung me away to cup his face, but I didn't have the strength to do more than brace.

Dvorak—both of him—wavered in my vision as Blay elbowed him in the jaw with a resounding *crack*.

"*Rue.*" He dove for me, catching me against his chest. "Blay protect Rue."

Before I could warn him, darkness swallowed me in a single gulp as Stavros rose behind him.

THE SMELL HIT ME FIRST, AND I NEARLY RETCHED AT THE STINK OF decomposition wafting on fetid air.

"Asa," I breathed, jerking upright only to get knocked back by a firm hand to my chest. "Where…?"

Sunlight beat down, coating my skin in sweat, and I recognized my surroundings with dawning horror.

"You're awake," a gruff voice grunted from beside me. "Good."

Two daemons moved into position, one on either side of me, and clamped my upper arms with bruising force. They growled every time I turned my head. They must have orders to make me watch the show.

I had been lying on a bench in the box where I once sat with Clay, and now I had a front row seat as Blay stretched and warmed up for the fight. His relief I was upright again was plain on his dear, sweet face.

A challenge was nothing to him. He was used to them. He fought. He won. End of story.

But this wasn't just *a* fight. It was *the* fight. One I had secretly hoped to avoid. For, I don't know, *forever*.

Each time I cut my eyes to search for the others who had gone to Hael, fresh misery stung them in bloodshot waves.

Without magic, even passive magic, I wasn't healing normally. I was mending human slow.

The one bonus was I still had my wand. Probably because no one thought a dowel was dangerous.

They must have never been caught in a craft supply duel between a golem and a moth.

I had, several times, and let me tell you. It was a quick way to lose an eye.

Static crackled through the air, the friction of magic and tech grating, and I focused on the field.

The same commentator as last time jogged out dressed in what must be his signature look. A red leather suit with black shoes. A gold lavalier mic pinned at his collar. A bodypack transmitter bulging at his spine. He was all polished smiles and smoothed lapels, pumped for a spectacle and ready for his performance.

His outfit, paired with his dusky orange skin and sleek yellow hair, made him resemble a living flame.

The flamboyant ensemble begged someone to dump a bucket of ice-cold water over his head to see if he would sizzle, but maybe that was just me. Captivity tended to make me cranky.

"You're in for a once-in-a-lifetime treat, creatures and creaturettes," he boomed to the empty stands. "Astaroth Xan Stavros, High Prince of Hael, will fight Orion Pollux Stavros, High King of Hael, Master of Agonae, for the crown of Hael." He drew out a dramatic pause. "To the *death*."

All battles were to the death, but I couldn't work up the energy to heckle him on technicalities. Not with these stakes. I craned my neck, which earned me a hard slap across the face from one of the daemons and almost made me vomit, but we remained alone.

Who was he posturing for? Why waste the showmanship? Who benefited from his antics?

"The show must be about to begin." I forced my knee to quit bouncing. "Is this a private viewing?"

It wasn't every day that a crown exchanged heads. Especially this one. Stavros had worn it for centuries. Hundreds of spectators could have fit on the benches and dozens more could have packed every inch of standing room. Yet the main portal was shut.

"The fate of a kingdom will be determined soon," a familiar rumbling voice informed me as heavy boots clomped up the stairs to where I sat. "These challenges are broadcast throughout Hael, for all to see."

Dvorak.

Given how cocky Stavros was about, well, *everything*, I shouldn't have balked to learn it was a live feed.

As if the thought had summoned him, Stavros prowled onto the field, shirtless and with his hair in braids that fell down his back. He stopped before Blay, who looked more bored from the waiting than anything else, and drank in the sight of him like it was the last time he expected to see his son. Alive, at least.

Desperation pushed me into a plea that had bad idea written all over it.

Okay, book. You've been begging me to use you for months. This is your chance.

The same persistent wall of nothingness blocked the fire in my veins, and the grimoire, muzzled by the restraints, remained quiet.

"Open your eyes." Dvorak pinched my thigh hard enough to bruise. "You don't want to miss this."

Until he mentioned it, I hadn't realized I had shut out the arena to focus.

"The battle for the throne begins..." the announcer pumped his fist, *"...now."*

Stavros landed the first punch so fast, I rose to my feet before my guards slammed me down again. I had never seen a daemon move like that, and my gut clenched with dread as the guards beside me cheered.

Blay wasn't as fast, but he fought to survive on a regular basis, and it showed in each punishing strike he landed as he grasped for Stavros's throat. I wanted to scream to forget his signature move, that it didn't matter how he won as long as he came out alive, but I couldn't risk distracting him.

"They're more evenly matched than I anticipated. Pity we won't know how it could have ended."

Unable to peel myself away from the carnage, I demanded, "What does that mean?"

A metallic bitterness clogged my nose as Dvorak twisted his fingers in a clockwise motion.

Magic.

He was working magic.

On Stavros?

"Ferrumae," he said casually. "You didn't ask, but that's my classification."

"Ferrum." I got a bad feeling in the pit of my stomach. "As in iron?"

"It exacts a toll each time I dare bend its will to my own." He gestured to his ruined face. "One day it will kill me for my hubris."

The next strike Stavros landed sent Blay staggering with an earsplitting bellow. Stavros cocked his head, glanced at his fists, then laughed out loud at whatever he saw. Dvorak shared his amusement, chuckling at the glee with which he pursued Blay across the field, raining down punishing blows with a cruel smile.

Oh goddess.

I tasted blood and realized I had bitten my tongue to keep from calling out to Blay.

What was I seeing? No, worse. What was I *missing*? What had put that smile on Stavros's face?

"No weapons are allowed on the field," he informed me, "but there are no rules against jewelry."

Blay staggered, gasping for breath, a hand on his ribs. His left eye was swollen nearly shut, and his cheek dented in. His jaw was wrong in an undefinable way, and he couldn't get his hands up to defend himself.

Oh goddess. Oh goddess. Oh goddess.

Only one thing hurt him that much. Cold iron. The base of Stavros's fingers gleamed with metal and…blood. Brass knuckles. No. *Iron* knuckles. A set for each hand, the top of each loop crowned with a spike. They must be retractable.

Forgetting the goddess, who didn't lift a finger to help, I prayed to the book instead. Not a great idea, to let a dark relic believe it was worthy of praise, but it answered in a rush of scalding eagerness.

Come on, book. This is your chance. Show me what you've got.

"This is cheating." I tried distracting him to give the book time to dissolve the barrier between it and me. "Stavros can't win if he cheats."

"He's not." Confident of his high king's victory, Dvorak settled back to watch. "I am."

As if Stavros didn't know. As if he couldn't tell. As if he wasn't aware his strikes landed with punishing finality.

Stavros executed a spinning kick that blurred reality as Blay was launched into the air.

He landed on the dirt in a heap of muscle. He wasn't moving. He wasn't breathing.

Neither was I.

For a beat, I couldn't find enough air to fill my lungs.

"Blay." I shot to my feet. "Get up right now, you hear me?" I struggled against the guards. *"Blay."*

Stavros palmed Blay's jaw in one hand then rested the other on his opposite temple in a parody of Blay's finishing move. His arms flexed as he prepared to snap his son's neck, but it was my patience that broke.

Goddess damn you, book. Get your ass in gear. Save him, or I won't stop until you cease to exist.

"Stop." I snapped my teeth at Dvorak like a rabid dog. "Whatever you're doing, stop."

Book, if you don't do something, I will tear out your pages and eat them one by one.

An anemic spark in my chest bloomed into searing heat that spread down my torso into my wrists.

The restraints sizzled, melting against my flesh and charring the air with burnt skin.

"Sire," Dvorak shouted a warning to Stavros. "The witch."

The cry jerked the guards' attention to me as they fumbled to resecure my hands.

"No." Dvorak swung his arm to strike me down. *"No."*

"Yes," I hissed, throwing back my head, the searing heat of a volcanic eruption of power scalding me.

CHAPTER FOURTEEN

"*D*ollface."

A hot, sticky weight clung to my skin, and I kicked my feet to get out from under a mountain of blankets. My bedroom was the hottest room in the house. I don't know why I always forgot to turn on the fan.

"Dollface." A warm hand touched my cheek. "Open your eyes."

A fuzzy throbbing in my head made me wince, and I tasted ash when I licked my dry lips.

"Colby is unconscious," a practical voice reported nearby, "but she's stable."

Fear thrummed through me as memories of the challenge kicked my heart into a gallop.

Jackknifing off the bed, I leapt to my feet, calves twitching, ready to run. "Asa."

Dark magic crackled between my fingers, hot and eager, its hunger sated but willing to feed again.

"Dollface." Clay caught me in a bear hug I had no hope of breaking. "We need to talk about Asa."

We need to talk.

Those words never ended well for their recipient.

"Wait." I finally identified the other presence in the room. "Dr. Nadir?"

"I understand you share a strong bond with your familiar." He kept his distance, his face drawn. "I came to verify with Mr. Kerr that it's normal for her to be affected by physical stress on you and your magic."

Clay sliced a hand through the air, silencing the doctor. "Do you remember what happened, Dollface?"

Stavros.

And Blay.

Oh goddess, Blay.

"You detonated in the arena." He eased me onto the bed until I sat beside him. "Ring any bells?"

"Yes." I couldn't breathe. There wasn't enough air. "Stavros had cold iron and—"

"We know." He kissed the top of my head. "The doctors are treating Ace for iron poisoning."

I was done sitting here. Done feeling helpless. Done listening instead of doing.

"Where. Is. He?" Panic slicked my brow with cold sweat. "Where is Asa?"

"He's in surgery. I brought in specialists for him. The best in their fields." Clay kept his chin pressed against me. "You can't see him right now."

"You can't stop me." I surged to my feet, unsheathing my claws. "Get out of my way."

So much wasted time, and now we might not have any. I should have mated him. I should have married him. I should have knotted us together in every way two people can be joined as one and then invented new ones. I should have burrowed under the covers with him and stayed there. Forever.

"Don't make me take you down." His fingers spilled open on his lap. "You know I hate putting hands on you."

During the years of our partnership, some of the darkest in my life, he had grown adept at defusing me. I would go on benders, too high on magic to control myself, and he was always there to stop me. With force.

He didn't enjoy the job, but he did it. Sometimes too well. Concussions via golem hurt like a mother.

Hence my expertise in self-diagnosing concussions. I had suffered a million of them.

A sharp prick stung my neck, and ice water floated through my veins in a cooling rush.

"I'm sorry, Rue." Dr. Nadir stepped back, lifting his hands at his sides. "We can't risk an episode here."

A syringe glittered between his fingers in the low light, but I held myself still rather than leaping on him and tearing his throat out with my teeth. I wish I could blame the grimoire for putting the idea in my head, but it was all mine. The only thing keeping me from coming unglued was feeling a power surge in my fingertips and knowing I could kill him, and everyone else on the farm, if I didn't get a handle on myself.

As a chill settled through my limbs and my head spun in widening circles, I was grateful to him.

"I…" I slumped onto my pillows. "I…"

"Don't fight it." Clay smoothed the hair from my face. "Get some rest, Dollface. I'll be right here, okay?"

Limbs heavy and growing colder, I murmured, "I need…a plan."

"Plans are good." He kept stroking my hair. "What kind of plan?"

A plan in case Asa didn't wake.

A plan to protect Colby if I broke.

The grimoire might contain theories on how to transfer a *loinnir* bond to another person. Aedan maybe. He would love her and keep her safe. Clay would be my first pick, if not for the director's sway over him.

Colby was too powerful to risk her falling into the wrong hands.

She wasn't a weapon or a tool. She was a kid. Just a kid.

She was *my* kid.

My little moth girl.

And…I couldn't leave her.

Even I wasn't that selfish, to abandon her in a world eager to prey on her light and goodness.

Moving on to Plan B.

Asa will recover, which means I will be fine, which means Colby will be safe, which means life goes on as usual, which means everything will be okay.

There.

Done.

As soon as I woke up, I would tell Clay, and he would agree it was a great plan. Excellent. The best ever.

Almost as good as whatever was in that syringe.

CHAPTER FIFTEEN

The sudden transition from asleep to awake startled a gasp out of me as much as opening my eyes to find Dr. Nadir standing over me with a pensive brow. He set the syringe down on the nightstand then held up his hands to show they were empty. He must have spent a lot of time working around dangerous people to have developed a bedside manner that balanced on the knife's edge between *I'm not here to kill you* but also *please don't kill me.*

"Sorry about that." He checked my galloping pulse. "We had to keep you out longer than anticipated."

"How...?" I coughed and choked on my dry throat, "...long?"

These frequent bouts of unconsciousness were starting to make me question my grip on reality.

"Sixteen hours." He flashed a blinding light in my eyes. "Mr. Kerr decided it was safest for everyone here if you slept through the worst of the uncertainty with Mr. Montenegro."

"I'm...going to..." I coughed again, "...kill him."

"Don't be too hard on him. He hasn't left your side the whole time." He aimed a pointed stare at the far corner. "Isn't that right, Mr. Kerr?"

"Thanks for outing me, Doc." Clay stepped into the light. "You did hear her threaten to end me, right?"

Amused by Clay's hesitancy, he assured him. "She's as weak as a kitten."

"A lion cub maybe," he muttered. "Don't murder me." He held up a bottle of water. "I'm going to lift your head and help you drink. Blink once if you understand me and twice if my days are numbered."

I blinked twice out of spite, which made him grin, but I wasn't mad at him for taking the necessary precautions. I was angry at the volatile situation and my inability to control it. "Asa?"

"Stable," Dr. Nadir reported. "He hasn't woken yet, but we have every reason to believe he will."

Moisture rolled down my temples, tickling my ears as they filled with tears. "Colby?"

"She's good." Clay cradled the back of my head in his massive palm. "She'll be over the second I give her the green light. We just wanted to make sure you weren't going to brutally murder me in front of her."

The first drops of cool water hit my parched throat, and I decided maybe I could let him live.

"Not so fast." He jerked the bottle back. "You don't want to vomit."

"Stavros?"

"Someone must have warned him." Muscles fluttered in his cheek. "He hit the portal, saved himself."

"Dvorak," I remembered, then cursed the daemon's quick thinking. "Callula?"

"A broken rib pierced her lung, but she's alive." He offered me more water. "Dvorak, however, is not."

"Good." I dribbled on my chin. "Moran deserves sole custody of Peleg."

"I couldn't agree with you more. For Dvorak to beat who he thought was Peleg that way…"

"Callula didn't break character." I wet my lips, but it didn't do much good. "She maintained her cover."

"She's a brave woman." He patted my mouth dry with a napkin. "So are you."

"Leandra? Cho?"

"Physically? She's healing. Mentally? She's struggling. Moran shielded her from the worst of what Dvorak, and his estate, had to offer. I don't think she realized how much so until now." He opened his mouth, shut it. "Cho..."

Waves of guilt crashed through me, and saliva pooled in my mouth. "What about him?"

"He has heartburn from eating too many pizza rolls." He dipped his chin. "He might not last the night."

Snatching the water from his hand, I dumped it over his bald head and laughed through his splutters.

"I prescribed him antacids," Dr. Nadir deadpanned. "I anticipate a miraculous recovery in the next hour."

"Leandra had burns." I touched my cheek, recalling the milky fluid dumped on us. "Will she scar?"

"The permanent damage is minimal and confined to her back."

A diplomatic answer if ever I heard one, but I read between the lines and wanted to help her heal.

I had asked her to confront her ghosts, so I had no right to act shocked when they spooked her.

"I'll see what I can do." I intercepted Clay's glare with one of my own. "*After* I recover."

"Mmm-hmm." He sniffed at me. "That's what I thought you said."

Toying with the label on the water bottle, I asked, "Anything else I'm missing?"

"Everyone saw you go boom, and I mean *everyone*." He hesitated. "The challenge was ruled a forfeit."

"Dvorak cheated first." I crushed the plastic in my hand. "He armed Stavros with cold iron."

"Be that as it may, thanks to extreme closeups, overhead shots, and wide-angle lenses, his manipulation was subtle. True movie magic." He rubbed his nape. "Yours...was more like the lone figure walking away from the huge explosion that killed everyone else."

"Stavros wants a rematch?" I made a guess. "Too bad." I snorted. "He's not getting one."

"Do you remember the first time you attended a match?" He

waited for my nod. "That assclown, Ruger, baited you to attack him, but I warned you Asa would forfeit if you struck his opponent?"

No one walked away from the arena. No one lived to fight another day. Challenges were to the death.

"No." A knot of dread stuck in my throat. "That's not…"

"Stavros has proof Asa cheated. That *you* cheated on his behalf. There were thousands of witnesses."

"I don't care."

"He won't let this go, Rue, and you know it. This is a prime opportunity for him to depose Asa without risking his neck in a fair fight. With Dvorak gone, we have no proof."

"Stavros wore cold iron—"

"—knuckles." He scrubbed a hand over his mouth. "Moran recognized the damage as Dvorak's signature."

"They were his?" I remembered now that he was ferrumae. "He must have loaned them to Stavros."

"That's our best guess. The knuckles are lined with gold to protect the wearer, which makes them more distinctive, but it doesn't matter. The evidence will be long gone before we can launch an inquiry."

"I had to make it stop," I whispered as reality struck me harder than Dvorak's boot. "I didn't care how."

For the first time, I had given myself over to the book, fully, and let it have its way with me.

"No one is blaming you." He stroked my hair. "You saved Asa's life, and that's what matters."

"For how long?" I pushed upright and leaned against my headboard. "How do I keep him safe?"

Thanks to me, his father could send his personal guards to fetch Asa for execution, and it would be valid.

Failing that, he could set a bounty on Asa's head, dead or alive, for anyone willing to drag him in.

Options got worse from there.

Much worse.

Warm hand cupping mine, Clay stared deep into my eyes. "We depose Stavros."

"Will that work?" A crown would suck, but at least Asa would have a head to wear it on. "Can Asa—?"

"Not Asa." His lips twitched to one side. "That ship has sailed right into the Bermuda Triangle."

"If we remove Stavros from power," I finally managed, "the new ruler will want Asa dead too. The kingdom will be vulnerable to a coup as long as he's alive. Who would be willing to take that chance?"

There was no way to win. No way out. We were stuck.

"Unless the new ruler has a vested interest in Asa's continued good health."

Try as I might, I couldn't scrounge up a single name for our possible savior. "Who?"

"Calixta Damaris," he said with a finality that convinced me he had dedicated long hours of research into our options and found her to be the least damning one. "The former High Queen of the Haelian Seas."

Her only vested interest in Asa's continued existence was as the mate of her heir: *me*.

Goddess bless.

When Clay told me we needed to think ahead, he must have been warning me he already had been.

And that I wouldn't like it.

"My *grandmother?*" I spluttered to recall our last meeting. "That's who you want on the throne?"

Knowing Clay, I ought to be glad he didn't expect me to steal the crown and grant Asa a pardon myself. Not that I could without an army. Not that I would when I was buckling under the weight of the title of Deputy Director. Black Hat was bad enough. I didn't need an entire kingdom dependent on me.

"Her throne was stolen from her. Her son was stolen from her. Her life was stolen from her."

The director had knocked her up, taken their child to raise in his image, then locked her in the swamp to rot, which cost her the crown of the Haelian Sea kingdom. Everyone thought she died mysteriously, not an uncommon event for royalty, a century earlier. But I knew better, and I knew right where to find her.

"Clay..."

"She wants freedom, revenge, and a return to power. Give her those, and she'll owe you a big favor."

Like overlooking how my mate was in line for the throne before she knocked him off the dais.

"I killed her mouthpiece and left her caged," I reminded him. "She's not going to shrug that off easily."

As far as she knew, she was trapped in there for eternity. Only blood of her blood could set her free, and I bested my cousin, her chosen champion. Delma and I had been the last of her line. Delma had killed off the rest to ensure she had no competition. Calixta didn't know I kept the ashes, that I could use those to release her. But I wasn't as sure as Clay that she would play nice after I snubbed her and ditched her.

"Offer her a throne and the director's balls on a silver platter, and she'll forgive and forget."

Eww.

I wasn't touching that second promise with a ten-foot pole.

If she had a hankering, she could harvest her own Rocky Mountain oysters.

"Or," I countered, "she might wait until my guard is down and kill us both."

End Asa, and the previous line of succession ended. End me, and she was free to pick a more loyal heir.

"Or that." He spread his hands. "It's the best I've got."

As far as plans went, I had to admit it wasn't... Okay. It was terrible, but I didn't have a better idea. "What are the rules of succession?"

"Let me bring in the professional." He made a quick call to Aedan. "He's been researching while you were sleeping to make sure what he recalled from his time in the Haelian Sea court translates to Hael."

"You've been busy." I was impressed with their dedication but not surprised by it. We were family, all of us, and we were in this together. "It's kind of nice to wake up to a plan for a change. Much less stressful than flying by the seat of my pants."

"Yeah, well, I figured your butt wings must be tired by now."

"They're exhausted." I jumped when the door flung open, the drugs making me jittery. "Hey, coz."

"Hey back." He fumbled armloads of handwritten scrolls. "I reached out to a few contacts in the Haelian Sea court to get their recollections of the last coup. The circumstances were different, but we've broken down the fine print and agreed the broadest translation of the laws allows for any—former, current, or deposed—monarch to challenge for any throne—vacant or occupied—that is without an heir or direct line of succession."

"Asa no longer qualifies." I dared nurse a seed of hope. "Stavros has no one."

"A high king or high queen of Hael aren't required to belong to a certain court or bloodline to hold the corresponding throne. Calixta can rule Hael if she can beat Stavros in an open challenge. Without Asa, he must fight for his crown for himself."

"And any battle against the king puts the crown in play." I fought back the excitement threatening to lift my spirits. "Do all coups involve reading so much fine print?" Now that we had a plan, I itched to set it in motion. "I thought a hostile takeover was a hostile takeover."

"We have to be smart about this. We can't leave Stavros an inch of wiggle room." Clay spread his hands. "We also can't allow Hael, or its people, to suffer without a fit ruler just to suit our agenda." He sat back. "Once the drugs are out of your system and you're thinking straight again, you'll agree. We want to protect Asa from retaliation, and this rips the target off his back."

"There's always been a target." Aedan spoke the ugly truth. "There always will be."

"I'll settle for normal levels of targetedness." I startled when he snapped a scroll open. "What's that?"

And how long did these drugs take to leave my system? Sheesh. Every noise or movement spooked me.

"A contract." He presented it to me, but I didn't have enough focus to read the words bouncing over the page. "These are the terms you're offering Calixta. I had Vestian check the wording for loopholes."

All that sounded good, but I wasn't sure when the farm picked up a lawyer. "Who is Vestian?"

"He runs Asa's household in Hael. He attended law school at Harvard and has the equivalent of power of attorney to manage the estate in Asa's absence." He tapped two bold black lines of empty space. "All that's left is for you and Calixta to sign."

We had come full circle. From Stavros and Asa to Calixta and me. Fate had a funny sense of humor.

"We figured a way out once." Clay squeezed my knee. "We can do it again."

The certainty in his voice anchored me as I felt the waters closing over my head.

"We don't have long before our flight." Aedan checked his phone. "We should leave soon."

"Leave?" I rubbed my temples, hoping to jumpstart my brain. "You expect me to leave Asa?"

"He's safer here." Clay primed his argument. "Even when he wakes, he won't be in any shape to fight."

He was right. I knew he was right. But I was terrified if I left, Asa would sense it.

I didn't want him to think I had abandoned him. Or given up on him.

I would never forgive myself if…

No.

Asa and Blay were going to be fine. Both of them. They had to be.

"Okay." I stunned them both when I let it go. "I'll pack an overnight bag."

"Already done." Clay recovered first, shooting me a wink. "I thought you'd see things my way."

"Especially if you laid out your plan while I was still high?"

"Yes," he agreed without a tinge of remorse. "That."

Aedan rolled up the contract, fastened it with a rubber band, and placed it on the bed.

"Let me grab my bag and tell Colby bye." He strode for the door. "I'll be ready in twenty."

The rest of what they weren't saying hit me, and I turned to Clay. "You're not coming."

Chicken that he was, Aedan slipped out before my anger splashed onto him.

"You think I believe for a hot second that you would go if I didn't stay to protect Ace?" He snorted at me. "I knew the drugs were good, but I didn't know they were *that* good."

Reading into his silence, I put the rest together. "You don't want to leave Colby alone."

Maybe there was a part of him that wanted to be there for Moran too.

"Plus, giant spiders."

"Plus," I agreed, "giant spiders."

Understandably, Colby wasn't eager to ever return to the place where one had held her hostage.

"You really did work it all out while I was sleeping." I stuck on a wobbly smile. "I should nap more often."

"That's what family is for, right?" He got to his feet. "Family also tells you when it's time to shower."

Mouth falling open, I gasped, "Are you saying I stink?"

"I did walk in here craving onions, if that's what you're asking."

"Sugarcoat it, why don't you?"

"The cold water will help wake you up. You need your head on straight before you confront Calixta." He stretched his arms over his head. "Oh, hey. I bought a blender for the communal kitchen. I'll have Aedan bring you a smoothie. He and Colby have been playing with it nonstop. No promises on flavors, though." He snickered. "Last I heard, he was experimenting with a banana kelp blend with bee pollen for crunch."

"Thanks." I swung my legs over the side of the bed. "For everything."

"You don't have to thank me. Ever. Especially not when it comes to taking care of you."

"I meant for protecting him." I battled vertigo to stand. "I wouldn't trust him with anyone else."

"I know what he means to you, Dollface, but we love him too. He's a good friend, and a good man."

After Clay left me to shower, I decided to skip cleanliness in favor of a more important task.

The thing I had learned about contracts was the devil was in the details. Or, in this case, the daemon.

Vestian might be the greatest legal mind with a pulse, but I knew a better lawyer without one.

Contacting Meg required time I didn't have, but I was trying to get better about not allowing impatience to force me into bigger messes to clean up later. That meant blocking out the few precious minutes I had to ensure my bases were covered before I butted heads with my grandmother.

Aedan wouldn't thank me for not taking his word, or a bath, but Meg was my gold standard.

And I owed her a Q&A session about Mom's condition. I had put it off since learning that Marita blabbed about Mom's return to Meg while bragging how she and Derry pitched in to help take down Old Man Fang. I had no excuse for not telling her myself, except that it hurt. Everything to do with Mom and Dad ached to the marrow in my bones.

The front door flung open, startling me enough to slosh water over the rim of the bowl I was filling.

"*Rue.*" Colby smacked into my back and clung. "Clay said it was safe to visit."

"Really." I sighed long and loud. "I hardly maim, maul, or murder anyone these days."

Except those guys in the arena, but they had it coming.

"Mmm-hmm."

"I need to contact Meg ASAP." I coaxed her onto my shoulder for a quick cuddle. "Be my lookout?"

"Sure." She flitted to the door then looked back at me. "We'll start by locking this."

Finishing up with my bowl, I told her, "That's why I brought in a professional."

Careful not to spill more, I sat cross-legged on the floor with the cool bowl cupped between my thighs. A sharp prick of my finger earned me the magical equivalent of a dial tone when my blood broke the surface.

"Megara, I summon thee." I squeezed out another drop. "Megara, I summon thee."

As usual, she refused to show until after I observed every formality, which could probably be blamed on her former occupation. She remained the best lawyer on either side of the veil, in my opinion, but death had impacted her business. Her fees were steeper, she was harder to contact, and she also required her clients to play secretary for her. There was no way around that when you hired incorporeal legal aid.

"Thrice I bid thee." More crimson plinked into the water. "And thrice I tithe thee."

The water began spinning in a slow counterclockwise circle as I ran a finger along the edge of the bowl.

"Hear me," I called in a resonant voice. "Arise."

Whirling gray wisps concealed Meg's features until the contents of the bowl turned smooth.

"You've looked better," she said, putting out her cigarette. "What's happened?"

"Oh, the usual." I played off the recent horrors to save on explanations. "Chaos and madness."

"That certainly describes those photos I saw of Derry riding that sea monster of yours." She huffed out a laugh. "That boy is so damn proud of himself." She chuckled. "However, that wife of his is steaming. You better come up with something equally idiotic for her to do if you want to balance the scales." She cast a knowing look at me. "You can't let one win all the time, or you risk losing both."

"Is this the equivalent of you telling me I better not break Marita or Derry's hearts *or else*?"

"There is no *or else*, not with you." Her sharp gaze softened on me. "I love you too much for that."

"I've already promised Marita to text her with a twenty-four-hour head start on Derry next time."

"That's the spirit." She cackled with glee. "That girl loves you like she loves chasing chickens."

A genuine smile sneaked up on me, but it wavered in the face of what I had to ask—what I had to say.

"I love you too." I set aside my wrenching heart. "I hate to rush you, but I don't have much time..."

"You won't rest until you're dead." She waggled her eyebrows at a second figure smudging the edge of the bowl. "Maybe not even then."

A man, one of many who called on her, must have realized this was a consult and disappeared to wait.

Heaven, for Meg, was all cancer-free cigarettes and consequence-free sex as far as I could tell.

Having already avoided The Mom Talk for weeks, I decided to consult her while her brain was sharpest.

"I'm hoping for a vacation between now and then."

"Doubtful." She waved her hand, sprinkling ash. "So, Little Miss Always in a Hurry, how can I help?"

Aware my time was limited, I gave her the short version that ended with a request for her services.

"That's quite the pickle." She crushed out her cigarette. "I remember the Maudit Grimoire." She drew in a breath then exhaled through her nose. "I prayed that wasn't what you had found, but that book knew a way back to its master when it saw one. Your father is the only author still alive. The book will do what it can to worm its way back into his possession." She tapped her finger. "Never tell him you have it."

"He knows." I cast my mind back to New Orleans. "After Lake Pontchartrain...there was no hiding it."

From the corner of my eye, I spied Colby ducking into the bathroom and emerging with her arms full of bottles, packets, and sprays.

"You can't trust him with objects of power. After what the director did to Howl, and you, the temptation to level the Black Hat compound and turn its agents to ash would prove too much." She reached out, but she couldn't take my hand from beyond the veil. "I'm sorry, Rue, but that book must be your burden. It's not fair or right, but you're strong enough to bear it. You have so much of your mother's goodness in you."

Just like that, my resolve to bring her up after our deal crumbled like a graham cracker crust.

"So, Marita told you about Mom." I fidgeted with the edge of the bowl. "Do you have any questions?"

"No." Meg studied me, chose a new cigarette, and flicked her lighter. "I'm up to date on the situation."

"Up to date?" I couldn't decide if that made me feel better or worse for being such a chicken. "How?"

"She's my best friend." Her tone made it plain I should have seen that coming. "Saint helped her ring me at the first opportunity. She and I have been talking a few times a day every day, and we will until..." She took a long draw that didn't satisfy, if her frown was any indication. "Until whatever happens, happens."

"I should have brought her up sooner." I winced at the copout. "I should have led with that."

"Don't look at me like that." She flicked ash off her sleeve. "I always knew your heart was soft, but you didn't always show it. These days, you can't hide it." Her smile gentled. "Don't feel guilty for prioritizing your situation. It's a smidge more time sensitive than hers."

"We don't know that." I forced myself to hold her stare and get it off my chest. "She could be gone tomorrow, and I didn't bother telling you she was back. I didn't even give you an opening to talk to me about her when I did call, because I wanted your mind free of distractions."

That wasn't good or kind or nice. That was selfish, petty, and mean.

"You're adorable." She crushed out her cigarette and put away the pack. "My mind is as sharp as a tack. That's one thing age and death haven't eroded." She set out a pen and paper. "I'm ready when you are."

Unrolling Aedan's hard work, I settled in to read to her. "Let the revisions begin."

We edited the contract in fifteen minutes flat. That had to be a personal best.

Aedan was right about Vestian's proficiency, but I didn't regret asking Meg for a second opinion.

"How will you juggle being the director's *and* Calixta's heir?"

"Good question." I wrote in her last suggested amendment. "The answer is—I have no clue."

They would fight over me tooth and nail, assuming he didn't outright kill me for freeing her.

"Well," she said, laughter deep in her throat, "as long as you have a plan."

"Am I doing the right thing?" I kept worrying why she got caged in the first place. "Releasing Calixta?"

"If your parents or your grandfather didn't want to risk her popping up again one day, then they should have killed her and been done with it. But they didn't, did they? They left her alive."

"That doesn't answer my question."

"All I can do is point out they made their choices, and now you have to make yours."

"Very fortune cookie of you." I dipped a finger in the bowl to send out ripples. "You've spent too long on the other side."

"Don't I know it." She smiled off to her left then wiggled her fingers. "Do you need anything else?"

"I don't want to keep you from an urgent appointment. Tell Mom I said hi the next time you talk."

"I'll do that." She focused back on me. "Don't let Derry and Marita drive you too crazy."

"I make no promises."

With that, she whirled away into nothing, leaving me with a clear bowl of water.

To avoid unwanted guests, I dumped it, rinsed it, and set it out to dry on the kitchen counter.

Ready to say my goodbyes to Colby, I turned and got sprayed in the face with dry shampoo. "Gack."

"You're fine." She brushed out my hair, paying my scalp extra attention. "Here." A plastic package hit me in the chest. Baby wipes. "Pits and privates." She hovered. "Also brush your teeth." She zoomed away to my closet. "While you clean up, I'll pick an outfit."

Five minutes later, I emerged from the bathroom dressed and smelling like a baby after a diaper change.

After kissing my little moth girl on her furry cheek, I rolled the amended contract tight and snapped on a rubber band. I slapped it once across my palm as I hit the steps.

Time to go swimming with my grandmother.

CHAPTER SIXTEEN

*W*e never did get around to relocating my grandmother. Probably to do with me learning my father was alive, that my grandfather had held him prisoner beneath the manor where he raised me, Mom returning as a vengeful spirit to murder me, and avoiding Stavros's overtures. There was also the promotion to deputy director, accidentally creating a new dark relic, and a million other things more important in the moment than figuring out how to move or where to stash a monarch no one—except me—seemed concerned about where she wouldn't be disturbed again.

Yeah, well, they would all be regretting their decisions to ignore Calixta Damaris soon.

The one good thing about Clay electing to stay behind was it allowed Aedan and me to hop a plane. The flight to Davie, Florida, took five hours. Even with a layover we couldn't avoid, it shaved five hours off the previous visit.

From the airport, it was a short drive in a rental to the Devlin Wildlife Center, the para-only sanctuary in northern Florida that had been selected for my grandmother's watery prison.

Florida, with its ample coastlines, abundant saltwater *and* fresh-water habitats, and tropical climate, was a popular dumping ground for the many paranormal creatures sold as pets on the black market after the poor beasts outgrew their enclosures, outgrew their cute phase, or outgrew their owners' patience.

Or if they ate a pet or a person. Sometimes both. Often more than one of each.

Basically, Florida was a great place to hide what you never wanted found.

Including, apparently, dethroned daemon high queens.

We parked our compact rental—another novelty—on the shoulder of the road and walked in.

Based on the warm ripple of power that washed over us, the perimeter defenses remained active.

That was good news. Very good news. Especially if this meeting didn't go as well as Clay anticipated.

As you would expect from a sanctuary home to dangerous other-worldly creatures that would kill you as soon as look at you, we rolled up on an entrance glamoured from human sight. A billboard filled with dire warnings in myriad languages greeted us past its open gates. The fine print stated you were on your own beyond that point, and that the sanctuary wasn't responsible for deaths, dismemberments, emotional trauma, or lost items.

Aedan strapped on a backpack charmed into an impenetrable shell to hide the contract and the ashes.

How he felt about carrying his sister's remains, I couldn't guess. His poker face was too good.

"Are you sure you want to do this?" He tossed a rock into the murky water. "We can find another way."

"There is no other way, or we wouldn't be here."

"Clay hasn't slept a wink since the challenge. He's been plotting like a madman."

"For the record, he never sleeps."

"You know what I mean."

"Yeah." I stepped into the brush. "I do."

The gates and the billboard were all that remained of the once popular attraction.

There used to be what seemed like miles of boardwalk stretching across the vast marsh. A visitor center too, for collecting admission fees that paid for the upkeep. But that was before Delma introduced me to our grandmother. Now the touristy amenities were gone.

I had burned them to the ground and watched them smolder.

"I should have brought a machete." I batted a cattail with my palm. "This is going to take forever."

When Aedan didn't respond, I craned my neck and found him fixated on where his rock had sunk.

"This is where she died," he said softly. "My sister." He touched the strap on his backpack. "I never paid my respects." His somber eyes lifted to mine. "Do you think that was wrong?"

I was no moral authority on right versus wrong, but my friends and my family tended to forget that with alarming frequency. I wasn't sure what absolution I could grant him with her blood on my hands and her ashes in an evidence baggie.

All I knew for certain about death was, if you were a black witch and you had embraced the dark arts, you simply quit one day. That was it. Over. Done. There was no *after*. No life. There was nothing.

For obvious reasons, I tried very hard not to think about that.

"You didn't owe your sister anything." I had no answers, so I told him a truth. "She wouldn't have cried over your grave, so why sniffle over hers?"

That might have come out harsher than I meant.

Because it was exactly what I meant, but I hadn't intended for him to know it.

"You're right." He waded in after me. "I just…" He dipped his chin. "I wish things had been different."

"We can light a candle before we go." I slapped a mosquito on my arm. "Say a few words."

"Do you even have a candle?" He pasted on a smile. "Or words for my sister that aren't expletive?"

"The gesture was symbolic."

"Mmm-hmm." He bumped his shoulder into mine. "Thanks anyway, coz."

152

The touch jarred him out of the past and into the present, and he stuck close as we ventured deeper.

A grassy river flowed around bald and pond cypress trees, slid underneath hardwood hammocks of live oak and gumbo-limbo. Ladies'-tresses orchids bloomed in nooks and crannies. The water churned with curious wildlife, mundane and extraordinary, going about their day with no interest in us. The moist air thrummed with insects, like the swarm of mosquitos sucking the life out of me one drop at a time.

"Calixta is out there?" Aedan slowed his march. "The High Queen is swimming around in...that?"

"I don't know how much swimming she can do, but she's here."

Our situation must be sinking in thanks to help from real-world visual aids.

"*This* is where you left her?"

A twisting undercurrent flowed beneath his words, and I was certain he was thinking of a different *her*.

Calixta had always intended for Delma to die, and I obliged her. As disposable as Delma saw her siblings, Calixta viewed her through the same lens. Aedan understood that, but I should have asked before tossing him a baggie of Delma's remains and expecting him to be okay ferrying it.

"I'm sure it's worse than it looks." I replayed that in my head. "Um, probably looks worse than it is?"

A snort blasted out of his nose, but he didn't contradict me, even if it was clear he wanted to comment.

Enough daemon court decorum lingered in him, or perhaps it was awe for a figure he heard whispers of his entire life, for it to not sit right with him that she was here. But a cage was a cage was a cage to me. I bet Calixta felt the same. Gilded bars, corroded bars, magical bars. It was all the same in the end.

"Do you ever worry this is how you'll end up one day?"

"No." I didn't have to think about it. "No one is stupid enough to lock me in and hope I don't get out."

They would kill me. Mix salt into my ashes. Scatter them to the four corners.

"True." He didn't have to think about it either. "You're too dangerous to have as an enemy."

"Aww." I pressed a hand to my chest. "You say the sweetest things."

"We have to uphold the family tradition." He batted a long fern out of his face. "Murder, betrayal, more murder, more betrayal." He sloshed closer to me. "And, to spice it up, even more murder and even more betrayal."

"We do have some awesome relatives, am I right?" I pictured our family trees. "Truly spectacular ones."

"Hall of Famers," he agreed with a twinge of regret. "Every one of them."

"We're not far now." I pulled out my phone to check our coordinates. "Just a few more minutes."

Fortunately, we'd had the forethought to mark the spot on a map app so we could find it again.

Unfortunately, we no longer had a way to reach it without going for a swim in water as thick as soup.

"You're a quarter Aquatae." Aedan must have caught my expression. "You can do this."

"I have no affinity for water." I trudged onward into the muck. "I must not have gotten the good genes."

"We can't all be so lucky." He slung an arm around my shoulders. "I'll promise you one thing."

"Just one, huh?" I squinted over at him. "What is it?"

"Anyone with a drop of Aquatae blood, even if the good genes skipped them, won't drown."

"Can I get that in writing?" I squinted over at him. "I've come close, like, a *lot*."

Most recently in Lake Pontchartrain.

A smile twitched on his lips. "But did you die?"

Now it was my turn to snort out a laugh, which ended in a choking fit as I sucked down a no-see-um.

Over my rasping inhalations, I heard a *click-click-click* that made my blood run cold and scanned the canopy.

Slowly, I drew my wand but kept it down at my side. "I thought you were dead."

"Um, Rue?" Aedan took a protective stance beside me. "Who are you talking to?"

An eight-legged nightmare the size of a small pony descended until it hung six feet above us. Its rounded body gleamed in oil-slick colors, its eyes opaque as moonstone, and chelicerae, pincerlike appendages, extended from its eager mouth. They click-clacked together, dripping ichor, and its fangs gleamed white.

"I am we," it told me. "We are many."

"That is a fucking huge spider." Aedan unleashed a full-body shudder. "Forgive the language."

"Colby's not here." I tightened my fingers. "And sometimes the truth needs saying."

It really was a fucking huge spider.

Ah, the F word.

Sometimes I felt my resolve to use polite language around Colby fizzle out like bubbles from the soap I promised to put in her mouth if she got salty with me. But, based on everything I had watched and read in a panic after bringing her home with me, kids shouldn't hear that kind of thing.

Don't eat the kid.

Don't let anyone else eat the kid.

Don't negatively expand the kid's vocabulary.

That was my original to-do list for Colby.

Easy enough place to start, right? Even I couldn't mess that up too badly.

"You are not welcome here," the spider whistled through its beak. "Leave this place and do not return."

"I'm here to visit Calixta." I lifted the wand for it to see. "I don't want to hurt you, but I will."

"We are many," it said with no small amount of confidence after spotting my crafting dowel. "We will not fail in our duties."

"You already failed once," I reminded it. "I was here, then I left, and now I'm back."

A rattling hiss filled the air between us as its anger sparked bright and hot.

"This is going to happen. You're either going to let it happen, or I'm going to make it happen. Your call."

A shiver in the treetops gave me my answer before it bared its glistening fangs and leapt at me.

Aedan knocked me face-first into the water, where I choked and spluttered, almost drowning.

Yeah.

I definitely got the short end of the water daemon stick.

A half dozen more spiders twirled on silken threads above us, rubbing their long front legs together with eagerness. These guys did *not* want to grant me visitation rights, but I wasn't leaving without a signature and my grandmother.

"How did you squish them last time?" Aedan yelled as he wrestled the beast. "Got a giant shoe handy?"

Shoving up out of the muck, I slipped and slid as I got my feet under me. I lunged for them and wrapped my hand around the spider's closest leg then shouted a warning at Aedan, "Think non-crispy thoughts."

Power roared up my arm, dark and hungry, and I was sick with relief that it came when I called. Magic ignited in my fingers, a creeping spread that rendered the vicious creature to ash, dusting Aedan like powdered sugar.

"Think non-crispy thoughts?" Chest heaving, Aedan pushed up into a seated position. "Really?"

"It worked, didn't it?" I jerked him to his feet, and we pressed our backs together. "Who's next?"

Wand at the ready, I steeled myself for an attack that never came.

The other spiders dangled from their webs, pincers clacking, but they didn't descend on us.

"Go," a smaller spider ordered to end the stalemate. "Leave this place."

"Do not return," another rasped, its beak clicking. "You are not welcome here."

"Did you not hear what I told your friend?" I watched them. "I'm not leaving, guys."

"You killed a giant spider on your first visit?"

"Yeah." I allowed my focus to drift to Aedan. "A few."

"The rest are much smaller." He squinted over our heads. "They're not as aggressive, either."

"Agree to disagree." I swung my attention back where it belonged. "What are you thinking?"

"They're not sentient." Aedan cocked his head, studying them. "Well, they are, but not like the big one." He dusted his shirt. "It held a limited conversation with us, but it's like the little ones spout prerecorded messages." He stepped forward, and the hissing rattles turned deafening. "I don't think they're a threat, not like the big one. Even then, I bet it was given simple instructions like 'if Rue does this, you do that' in escalating tiers until its programming determines if your trespass merits death."

"They're NPCs."

"You remembered." He grinned. "Yes, they're NPCs."

Nonplayable characters. Bits of code that ran in a loop. Except, in their case, the code was a spell.

"If you're right, then I feel bad." I dusted black residue off his shirt. "I killed all the smart ones."

"I'm sure the dozens of little ones spinning over our heads will grow into big ones one day."

"And just like that, I no longer feel bad."

"Glad I could help alleviate your guilt."

"Does this mean we can ignore them?" I doubted you could mentally block out so many spiders, but I was willing to try. "Or outsmart them?"

Without incinerating the entire swamp, I wasn't sure I could protect us from so many creepy-crawlies. That was a surefire attention-getter, so I preferred avoiding that route. The last thing I wanted was to give Black Hat, or anyone else, a reason to turn an eye to this area and what was hidden within it.

All I needed was for the director to put in a surprise appearance and catch me liberating Calixta.

"I want to believe I'm smarter than a spider," he said, "but I've also never seen one so big I could ride it."

"Here goes nothing," I murmured to him then called out to the spiders. "We're leaving, and we won't come back." I let them absorb that, and they retreated a fraction to show good faith. "But we parked that way." I pointed across the swamp. "We'll have to swim to get to the car." That earned me annoyed hisses and snarls. "It's the fastest way to get rid of us. Otherwise, we'll be tromping around and murdering you guys for hours."

Surely, after so long, they knew where visitors arrived in this place. But there was also a chance that, as Aedan theorized, they were simple creatures programmed with if/then solutions to problems. The small ones might not even have that much to rely on.

If I offered to leave, *then* they would probably let us go.

If they figured out we were lying, *then* they might very well eat us.

The creatures conferred above us before the largest remaining spider slid down its string to stare me in the eye. "Go." Pedipalps unfurled toward me before withdrawing. "Do not return."

A spark of hope that Aedan was right, based on their limited vocabulary, had me willing to risk it.

"Thank you." I dipped my head in a show of respect. "We'll be out of your hair in a minute."

The app flashed a bright-red pin, and I shared the vicinity with Aedan before reorienting myself.

Aedan, after shedding his human glamour, wore his blue skin with his fancy gills and dove in first.

"Showoff," I grumbled, sloshing until the warm water hit my chest before swimming after him.

Earthy rot and fresh decay stuffed my nose, but I tuned them out to focus on pinpointing the cage.

Without the boardwalk, which I now regretted vaporizing, I

couldn't check my phone to be sure I hadn't deviated from my path. I could have fished it out of my pocket, but then I would have begun sinking, and I really didn't want to snort whatever made the water smell as ripe as troll breath.

A yelp up ahead told me Aedan had done me the favor of locating the wards.

Too bad he had spawned a new problem. He was stuck like a fly on flypaper, the same as Blay had been. The harder he yanked on whatever the ward had grabbed, a foot most likely, the lower he sank. He was in no danger of drowning, but I didn't trust Calixta not to take a nibble if I didn't get him free before she caught scent of him.

"Hold on." I swam to him, careful not to get too close. "Does it have your foot or your leg?"

"My big toe."

"Your big toe." I watched him flail. "That's it?"

This wasn't the time to laugh, but goddess. I had reached my limits. The Colby drama, the Hael drama, the Stavros drama. Now this. I was drained to the point that pesky little voice in my head voted I bite into the nearest heart like a ripe apple for the energy boost to make it through this mess.

I won't lie. I was tempted. Part of me always would be.

Until it hit me.

The nearest beating heart belonged to my cousin.

That wasn't me. Not anymore. No matter how bad it got, I wouldn't stoop that low.

And I sure wouldn't break my diet starting with Aedan.

"I'll get you free." I gripped his shoulder to anchor me. "Just try not to kick in my teeth, okay?"

Using his torso as a handhold, I dragged myself lower, until duckweed teased my nostrils.

"Wait." He went pliant in the water. "Comms charm?"

"Good idea." I quit kicking and spun until I located a tender green vine. "Here goes nothing."

I broke a curling length in two, tied one piece around his neck, then knotted the rest around mine.

Waterlogged, I had no choice but to lean on the grimoire for a boost to overcome my submersion.

The dark magic leapt to my fingertips, eager to be of service, and I swear I felt the book smile.

With almost no resistance—not good, not good at all—the comms charms affixed themselves to our throats.

Now we could hear each other, as well as any conversation held within a short range of one another.

Using his torso as a handhold, I dragged myself down to Calixta's lair. Just as I had with Blay, I fed power into Aedan, drawing on that core of goodness from Colby, until he luminesced around me. With so many miles between my familiar and me, I had to work harder to reach her light. That, and using the book had smudged my powers with darkness. Her magic struggled to shine through the sooty window of my soul.

As my lungs burned with their last dregs of air, the ward shied away from that taste of white magic and spat him free. The brightness stung my eyes, but in the deepest shadows, I made out mounds of bones in all shapes and sizes. The grim debris loomed higher than last time, the crushed skulls grinning.

The older skeletons, the ones at the base of her cell, took on a horrid new dimension as I reflected on my conversation with Aedan. Those were relatives of hers. *Ours.* People I never met and never would.

Clearly, I had inherited my tendency to eat my feelings from Calixta.

Faster than I registered the shift in the current, a slender hand shot through the bars, and fingers cruel as a garrote wrapped around my throat and squeezed bubbles past my lips.

"Hello, Granddaughter." Calixta remained ageless, beautiful, and borderline feral. "Come for a visit?"

Vision darkening on its edges, I gurgled a response that left me lightheaded from oxygen deprivation.

"Found a use for me, have you?" Her gaze bored into mine. "A reason to come crawling back?"

What did it say about our family that we used one another until trading favors was our only value?

What did it say about me that, as much as I hated being used, I was doing the exact same thing?

Goddess, familial relationships were a nightmare to navigate. Like wandering a maze blind while hoping the minotaur didn't kill you before you reached the center. Except the maze was the relationship, and the minotaur was whatever family member you were trying to negotiate a truce with before they devoured your heart or picked the flesh off your bones or stuck you in a watery cage for eternity.

A thin stream of expelled air tickled my cheeks as it fizzed out of my mouth on a *yes*.

"What could you possibly have to offer that would deem you worthy of my forgiveness?"

"A…" instinct urged me to gulp for air, but that would only drown me quicker, "…kingdom."

"I don't want *a* kingdom." She shook me until my eyes crossed. "I want *my* kingdom."

A firm hand closed over my shoulder, and Aedan sank until his head was level with mine.

"Release her." He held a short blade in his hand. "She can't bargain with you if she's dead."

"Penton?" Her punishing fingers relaxed as her face went slack. "I thought…"

Pretty sure Penton was Aedan's grandfather, her former lover.

"Forgive me, Majesty." He inclined his head in a respectful bow. "I must bring her to the surface."

Looping his arm around my waist, Aedan kicked with forceful strokes, shooting us toward the sunlight. We breached behind a cove of tangled cypress roots with knobby knees that gave me secure handholds.

After I coughed up a lung, I caught my breath and found Aedan scanning the canopy for movement.

"Are you good here?" He floated easily. "Our eight-legged friends will see you if you climb back on land."

"I can manage." I held on tighter. "This is why you wanted to come, isn't it?"

"How else could we negotiate with her?" He smothered a grin. "Don't make that face. It's not your fault. You've got a lot on your mind. You can't be expected to think of everything yourself." He chucked me on the chin. "That's why you have us."

The wind teased my damp hair, swirling the pungent rot of black magic around me.

Colby had been cleansing me with her light, wiping my slate clean, but The Hunk was a dynamic weapon. A dark instrument that drew on the blood staining a witch's hands and their moral decay. The more magic I took from it, the more darkness it gave me. I could smell it now. On my hands. In my hair. On my breath.

A jolt of worry shot across his features. "Rue?"

"Don't get too close to her." I dismissed his concern to justify ignoring my own fears. "Watch your back."

An argument brewed in the set of his jaw, but he let it go. He had no choice. Calixta was waiting, and royalty never did that for long.

"I have more toes if things get sticky," he joked, but it fell flat. "Keep an eye on the canopy."

"Oh." I tipped my head back. "I will."

While Aedan sank until I couldn't see him, I made myself as comfortable as I was likely to get in present circumstances. With my back to the cypress, I had some protection. From here, I could watch for spiders above me and goddess-only-knows-what swimming around me.

Calixta was the greatest threat in residence, but she was also the tip of the iceberg.

Other dangers lay in wait, unseen beneath the surface.

Across the way, a pair of bright-red orbs set in a knotty black face emerged from the water.

A makara.

That was what Colby called it before telling us it had ten legs and three mouths.

Seconds later, it seeped back underwater, leaving me uncertain if that made me feel better or worse.

"Testing," Aedan said in my ear, jolting me out of my vigil.

"I hear you, loud and clear."

"You forgot to say over."

"Do people really say that?" I smiled at our old joke. "I hear you loud and clear, over."

A few seconds passed while he reached the proper depth, and my heart thundered in my ears the entire time.

"Not Penton, then," Calixta mused. "And too young to be a grandson of mine." Her tone became thoughtful. "Are you the gift she wishes to give me? An apology made flesh?"

The hunger in her question turned my stomach into a churning sea. I hadn't considered she might view Aedan as a replacement for one of her favored consorts. They had no blood ties, but still.

Ick.

"No, Majesty." Aedan kept his address formal and respectful, and the ease with which he slid into a subservient role made my eye twitch. "I am here to facilitate the discussion between yourself and your heir."

"She's no heir of mine," Calixta snarled with disgust. "What heir would leave their queen to rot?"

"Pretty much every heir I've ever met," I muttered, glad only Aedan could hear me snipe.

"Apologies," he murmured. "I misspoke."

"I do like you. I like your pretty face even more. However, I *dis*like being used."

"Your granddaughter wishes to come to a mutually beneficial agreement with you."

"You have such lovely manners. Penton was the same. Such an elegant man." Her laughter turned sultry. "Do you know I was once paid the weight of my prized orcaella brevirostris stud, Arnaut, in gold for one night of Penton's service? I couldn't bear to share him, not fully, but I did offer his admirer the use of his tongue for an hour."

I heard her smile. "He would be proud of how beautifully you've turned out."

About to throw up in my mouth, I prompted him, "Get to the overthrowing-the-kingdom bit."

"The High King of Hael was challenged by his son and heir, Astaroth Xan Stavros, and the match was ruled a forfeit." Aedan hurried to snare her interest. "Allegations were made that both Asa *and* Stavros cheated, but there was enough evidence against Asa for Stavros to publicly denounce him as his heir."

"The line of succession has been broken," she mused. "That leaves Stavros vulnerable to challenge from any who qualify to rule."

"Meaning you could claim the High Throne of Hael in a bloodless coup."

"Coups are never bloodless," she clipped out then asked, "What are my granddaughter's terms?"

"Rue asks that, in exchange for releasing you, you dethrone Stavros, claim the High Throne of Hael as yours, and publicly decree Asa is under your protection."

"Not good enough." She dismissed him out of hand. "What use have I for Hael?"

"You are a queen," he said diplomatically, "and every queen requires a throne."

Hael might not be the Haelian Seas, but it was a step up from Queen of the Swamp.

"I yearn for the open oceans, the bite of saltwater, the give of brined flesh between my teeth."

"The High Queen of the Haelian Seas is vulnerable to your reappearance."

"Aedan," I whisper-screamed his name. "This was not part of the script."

"Oh?"

"Even those who sided with her during the ascension did so believing their rightful queen was dead."

"Are you listening to me?" I demanded. "We didn't say anything about a two-for-one special."

Championing one new monarch was risky, but plotting to over-throw two kingdoms was lunacy.

"That is most gratifying to hear."

"She holds the upper hand, for now, as the one who sits on the throne. If she were to discover you're alive, and—goddess forbid—where to find you, she will kill you. Unless you bargain with Rue, if that day comes, you'll still be trapped like a fish in a barrel."

"Oh?" A thoughtful hum filled the space between them. "That sounds almost as if you'd tell the imposter queen my location if I deny my granddaughter's request. And here I thought we were becoming friends."

"Apologies for my lack of diplomacy." He didn't deny it. "Our urgency has cost me my manners."

"How does seizing Hael further my goal of reclaiming my throne?"

"Once you rule Hael, you will have the resources at your disposal to retake your rightful place."

"Aedan," I tried again. "You're talking about starting a war between Hael and the Haelian Seas courts."

"A queen alone cannot hold two such vast kingdoms. It has been tried many times in the past by queens and kings alike. All attempts to unite the daemons under a single crown have resulted in destruction and death, chaos and misery. I do not wish that to be my legacy."

"Then relinquish Hael's throne after yours has been reclaimed."

The potential simmered with possibilities that caused a nail-biting lapse in their discussion.

"I could, perhaps, name a proxy." She toyed with the idea. "I could seat my heir on Hael's high throne after I have reclaimed mine."

Dread crashed through me in an icy wave at the choices unfurling before me.

Either I claimed the throne I had cost Asa, or I risked losing my best chance at keeping him alive.

"I'll do it." I didn't have to think about it. "Tell her, I'll do it."

"Rue agrees to take up the mantle." Aedan finally listened to me. "She is willing to—"

"How could I trust her?" Calixta laughed, the sound dark and

165

unforgiving. "She's proven herself as sly as her grandfather and every bit as much of a liar. No. Rue won't do. Not for this."

"She defeated Delma in battle," he reminded her. "She won the appointment in combat."

"A challenge no one witnessed except for those who would benefit from that knowledge not spreading."

That wasn't as much of a deterrent as she might think, given who else was aware of my position.

"The director knows," I warned him. "He knows she named me as her heir."

And then he pitched a tantrum over how I was his, not hers, when I wanted nothing to do with either of them or their legacies.

"Majesty?" Aedan, again, chose to ignore me. "You sound as if you have someone in mind."

"Delma was your sister. It's well known she was hunting her own bloodline to cement her claim. Let the world believe she challenged you, her final hurdle. Let them believe you won. With allies such as yours, it's not an unbelievable outcome."

"Majesty…" A tremble shook his voice. "I…"

"You are descended from a most beloved consort," she coaxed. "Who would question your quest to restore your queen to her rightful place? No one. And, after defeating your sister, my former heir, it's only right you take her place. To succeed where she failed me."

"*No.*" I shoved off the cypress, ready to take a plunge. "You're not taking a hit like that for me."

"In exchange for freeing you, and me taking Rue's place as your chosen heir, you'll sign the contract and launch a coup against Stavros? You'll allow Asa to live?"

"Give me your loyalty," she promised, "and I will agree to all other terms."

"Don't you dare," I threatened him. "She'll take me, or she'll stay sunk."

"Consider it done," he said too fast to have truly comprehended he was signing his life away.

"Rue?" Her voice drifted up to me, confirmation she knew I was listening. "Do you agree to my terms?"

The water must still obey her small magics, creating a conduit for us to have this conversation.

"No," I answered for myself. "That's not the deal on the table."

"Rue," Aedan said softly in my ear. "I was raised in and around the daemon courts. I know their ways. I have a better chance of surviving this than you do." He exhaled. "Let me do this for you. You saved my life. I owe you."

"You don't owe me anything. We're *family*. That's not how this works."

"I didn't expect to live this long." His confession cut my heart in two. "I wouldn't have without you."

"That doesn't mean your life is mine to toss in a flaming dumpster fire."

"I got to be free, for a little while. Normal. I had a family. I made friends. I found..."

He bit off the name, or maybe what she meant to him, but I understood too well.

Arden.

He meant Arden.

And his appointment to heir meant never seeing her again.

This was too much. The sacrifice was too great. I had to make him see reason.

"Funny how your definition of family extends to a cousin with no blood relation, who you would sacrifice even yourself to save," Calixta interrupted us, "but not to your grandmother, who you would bind in contracts before lifting a finger to help."

"Aedan has earned his place in my family. Family isn't blood. It's love. It's trust. It's not a bargain struck."

"You have bigger responsibilities than this," he murmured to me. "Smaller ones too."

Colby.

That was who he meant.

She was both the biggest and smallest of my responsibilities.

And she would never forgive me if I gave up Aedan to save myself.

"You're my responsibility too." I choked on a well of emotion. "I love you, Aedan."

"I love you too, coz." He exhaled with determination. "That's why I'm doing this."

"Grandmother," I addressed my next plea to her directly. "Please."

"Are you crying for him?" Calixta mocked the break in my voice. "Are you mourning him?"

Mourn.

There would be tears aplenty if I came home without him.

And one mourner, when she realized he was gone, would never forgive herself…or me.

Things hadn't ended well between him and Arden, but I wasn't sure they had really ended at all.

"What will I tell *her?*" I knew it hit below the belt, and I didn't care. I lined up for another swing anyway. "She'll ask about you one day, and what do I say?"

"That she's safe from monsters," he answered woodenly. "That this one won't darken her door again."

Fear he viewed this as an escape, that he was doing it for Arden, left me frantic to break through to him.

"You've worked so hard to free yourself from daemon politics," I protested. "Don't throw it away."

"Do you require her word," Aedan asked Calixta, his mind made up already, "or will mine suffice?"

"Vow to me that you will be my heir, that you will fulfil your obligations as if you were my own son, and I will allow your word to stand for hers."

"I will be your heir," he repeated. "I will fulfil any and all obligations you see fit to assign me."

"Please, Aedan." I couldn't see a way out, and he wasn't even looking. "Don't do this to yourself."

"You gave me a place to call home and people to love as family," he countered. "All I'm doing is applying what you taught me."

"Why would you do that?" I challenged. "I'm making it up as I go along."

"That makes two of us." I heard the smile in his voice. "Tell everyone back home I'll miss them."

"I won't have to," I rasped, done with hiding. "I'm not leaving without you."

Torturous seconds passed during which I heard nothing else from him, or from Calixta.

Convinced the charm had fizzled out, I filled my lungs with air and prepared to dive for him.

When Aedan breached in front of me, his hair slicked to his scalp, I made a noise like a deflating balloon and slung my arms around his neck. He returned the embrace fiercely, burying his face in my shoulder.

When he withdrew, waterdrops tipping his lashes like tears, it was to present the contract to me.

Calixta had signed her name in curling script.

So had he, on the line meant for me.

"I'm sorry." He kissed my cheek. "Bye, Rue."

The rib-bruising force of the palm he smashed into the dead center of my chest sent me flying backward. I cracked my skull against the wall of roots, too stunned to defend against his sudden act of violence.

"Aedan," I screamed, black dots glittering on the edge of my vision. "*No.*"

He had the ashes. Delma's ashes. He wouldn't dare—

Light erupted in front of me, illuminating the bars of what had been an invisible cage. Laughter rang out, a dark contrast to the bright magics devouring the construct whole. The power scalded my skin, and the water boiled around me. To keep my flesh from cooking, I reached for the grimoire again. Its delight was a fingernail dragged down the chalkboard of my eroding conscience, but it flung out a spherical ward to encase and protect me.

Perhaps to reward my newfound dependency, it took it a step further and began filtering oxygen from the surrounding water so I could breathe. I was leaning more on its power to keep my heart pumping, and its insidious whispers crept through my mind, reminding me how glorious it had been, once upon a time, to feast on fresh hearts. How together, it and I could topple the magical worlds.

The slippery slope that had been imminent since I picked up the grimoire?

Yeah.

I was sliding down it so fast now I couldn't tell which step had been the wrong one.

"Thank you." Calixta materialized from the darkness to hover outside my bubble. "For the gift."

"He's not a gift." A snarl revved up my throat. "He's—"

"Mine." Her smile flashed shark teeth. "Don't worry, Rue. I'll take good care of him." She tapped a finger against Aedan's throat, and a silver collar locked in place. "He's so lovely, isn't he?"

"Take it off him," I demanded. "He's not a pet."

"The torque is traditional," he assured me, his fingers tracing the thick band. "A symbol of my station."

"Heirs don't usurp their betters in my kingdom." She snapped her fingers and a second collar appeared in her hand. "There are consequences to disobedience under my rule. Care for a demonstration?" She brushed her thumb across its surface. "It might prove instructional for you both." Four-inch spikes exploded from the band. "Remember this moment after you've gotten what you wanted for yourself. Before you get any pesky ideas about liberating him from our bargain, I want you to look me in the eyes and believe me when I tell you I will slit his throat before I release him from service."

"Out of spite."

"What do you think has kept me alive this long?"

"It's okay, Rue." He pressed his hand against the bubble. "I'll be fine."

A kernel of anger burned its way through me, hotter than the broil around me, but I bit the inside of my cheek to keep from vowing I would come for him, that I would set him free if it was the last thing I did in this life. Instead I fit my hand within the outline of his and made a silent vow I willed him to hear.

"He will be content in my court," Calixta purred. "He will learn at my knee what pleases me."

The phrasing turned my stomach, and I didn't hide it well based on her smug grin.

So much for *as if you were my own son.* That lasted all of five minutes.

"As much as I would love to savor this role reversal of you trapped behind a barrier in my prison, my heir and I have plans to make and kingdoms to topple." She patted his cheek then screwed up her features at me in consideration. "I would wait a few hours before climbing out of that bubble if I were you, darling."

That explained the boiling-seas routine. Aquatae could handle it, but she wanted to ensure I didn't chase her down, filet her like a fish, and take my cousin back. And I would. Regardless of the consequences.

Which would land us right back in hot water. Though maybe not quite *this* hot.

"We'll be in touch." She wiggled her fingers in a wave. "Come on, Aedan. Let's not tarry."

With a flick of her wrist, an unspeakable force slammed the bubble against the cypress knees. I bounced hard, and my head smashed into the barrier, aggravating the injury Dvorak had dealt me. Her hand as she braceleted Aedan's wrist was the last thing I saw before my eyes rolled back in my head.

CHAPTER SEVENTEEN

*C*ool fingers brushed across my forehead, and I blinked awake on my back under a full moon.

"Hey, baby." Mom kissed my cheek. "You're going to be just fine."

For several heartbeats, I convinced myself I was dreaming, that she was a figment of my imagination.

But if I were going to dream her, it wouldn't be with her skin faintly sticky with ectoplasmic goo.

Or with me soaked to the bone, nursing a throbbing headache, and smelling like dead fish.

I had been hit in the head a lot lately.

Maybe this was brain damage talking.

"Don't baby her, Howl." Dad leaned over me. "Do you have any idea what you've done?"

"She only did what you would have done." Mom threaded her fingers through mine in a show of support that made my chest swell with a different type of ache. "She saved her mate's life, at any cost."

The jump in logic from *free granny* to *save Asa* wasn't far, given how widely broadcast the challenge had been. Mom and Dad would have kept an ear out for news of Asa and me. The grapevine must be

172

buzzing with gossip about what I had done, what Asa had lost, and what Stavros would do next.

Hand sliding through his blond curls, he raged, "That's no excuse."

"You made an animus vow," I reminded him. "You chose to die rather than live without Mom."

A vague recollection of a similar notion drifted to the surface of my thoughts, and I cringed at how much I was my father's daughter. I had gotten lucky. Asa was stable. He would recover. Blay would too. But at my lowest, I had stared into the void of my future and been tempted to step off the ledge into darkness.

Gah.

I didn't want to sympathize with Dad. I didn't want to understand him. Maybe even forgive him.

With my family looking to me as an example of *what to do*, instead of *what not to do*, I had to do better.

For them.

For me too.

"How did you know where to find me?" I scanned the canopy with a tickle of dread. "The spiders?"

"You destroyed my construct," Father snapped. "I was alerted the instant it collapsed on itself."

Had I been in my right mind, it might have occurred to me he would come running when I knocked down his house of cards. But I had been too frantic over Asa, and then Aedan, to worry about one more thing.

"We saw the spell you cast," Mom ventured, ever the diplomat. "You still have the grimoire."

"Or it has her," Dad grumbled. "Honestly, Rue, what were you thinking?"

"You'll have to be more specific." I planted both palms in the wet soil and leveraged myself into a seated position so he wouldn't be lording over me quite as much. "Which part?"

"The more you use the grimoire, the more you'll *want* to use it. You'll lean on its knowledge, its power, until it's all that props up your magic." He paced to the water and back. "How could you be so foolish?"

"Hmm." I tapped a finger on my chin. "It's almost like if I'd had a father to teach me right from wrong, I might have made different choices in my life." A low blow, yes. He hadn't chosen to be a captive, but the hurt over his decisions made it hard to care what I said as long as it hurt him back. "When you fix the hot mess that is your life, then you can lecture me on mine."

"Must you two always bicker?" Mom tutted at us. "You're too alike. That's the problem."

Both of us made huffing noises that amounted to the same thing —*No, we're not.*

Mouth thinned to an annoyed slash across his face, he asked, "What were your terms with Mother?"

"*Saint.*" Mom swatted him. "Leave her alone."

"What?" He appeared genuinely baffled at her rebuke. "She's recovered her senses."

"Meg—" I began, but Mom cut me off there.

"See?" She aimed her triumph at my father. "She used Meg. That means the terms will be favorable."

"*If* Calixta had accepted them as written, yeah." I hated to burst her bubble. "They would have been."

"See?" He jabbed a finger at me. "She had an ironclad agreement and couldn't close the deal."

Mom tucked her hands under her thighs like that was the only way to force them to behave.

Hmm.

So that's where I got my short temper and tendency to smack my loved ones upside the head.

"You're right, Dad. I screwed up. Big time." I flicked a weed off my cheek. "Does that make you happy?"

Confusion pinched his features, and he crouched before me. "How could your pain ever please me?"

The fight drained out of me as my new reality sank in, and he must have read the defeat on my face.

"What did she take?" He set his hand on my shoulder. "How can we help?"

How can we help?

That offer might have meant something had he made it sooner.

But it was too late.

"As punishment for abandoning her," I told them, "Calixta disinherited me."

"That's good news." Mom tipped up my chin with her fingertip. "Why are you so upset?"

Dad watched me, really looked at me, and I could tell the instant he understood what had been taken.

"Calixta named my cousin, Aedan, as her heir." A tear rolled down my cheek that I ignored with everything in me. "Aedan did it...for me." Another tear joined the first. "He thought he owed it to me."

"Come here, baby." Mom wrapped me in her cold embrace and rocked me. "I'm so sorry."

"Don't give up hope." Dad awkwardly patted the top of my head. "We can figure a way out of this."

"I've lost him," I hiccupped on a sob. "Now I can't get him back."

I sounded like a small child, one who wished her parents would swoop in and fix everything with a wave of their wands. But magic didn't work like that. Often, neither did parents.

Expression distant, he rose and began pacing again. "How about a trade?"

"A trade?" I scrubbed my face dry with the backs of my hands. "That defeats the purpose."

Anyone else she would accept from me would cost just as dearly and spit in the face of Aedan's sacrifice.

We would be no better off than when we started, and I couldn't play musical chairs with my family.

"Mother took Aedan to hurt you. She doesn't care about him one way or another." He ignored my glare, his distant gaze on the horizon. "Offer her a prize who matters to *her*, a bargain *she* can't resist, and she might trade." He looked at me then. "Revenge is a powerful lure."

"I don't know." Mom got there before I did. "Do you think that's wise?"

"The director." I read between the lines. "That's who you mean."

"You can't keep sitting on the fence." Dad brushed a curl off his forehead. "You have to pick a side."

"I was never on his side." I couldn't believe I had to break it down for him. "It's the Bureau that concerns me." I hated admitting it, knowing he would view it as proof of toeing the company line. "I've signed my first agents. Teen girls who didn't have any good options. I was the best of the bad ones."

Markus and Trinity Amherst didn't count. The black witch siblings had deployed the Boo Brothers' spirits as their personal hitmen and participated in a summoning ring that cost innocent people their lives. As if that wasn't bad enough, they also helped my predecessor raise Mom under a compulsion to murder me.

However, Tibby Garnier, the last living Lazarus witch, and Eliza Toussaint, her girlfriend, saw Black Hat as a sanctuary. A place where they could be themselves, together, safe from their families and persecution.

I sold them on that vision, and now I had to pay up.

"You?" She cocked an eyebrow. "Not Black Hat?"

"You know what I mean." I dared peek at Dad, but he had gone silent. Probably biting his tongue to keep from snarling at me. "I can't sign them then abandon them. They're my responsibility."

Over my head, Mom and Dad exchanged a weighted glance that gave away nothing of their thoughts.

"What's with the looks?" I used the tree to stand. "What are you thinking?"

"Worry about the Bureau later," Dad said at last. "For now, we need to focus on how to get Father outside the compound long enough to neutralize him."

"*We?*" I expected him to contradict me. "You mean you're going to stick around and help for once?"

"I've convinced your father," Mom spoke over my snark, "to spend what time I have left as a family."

"Ah." I couldn't catch the words before they flew out of my mouth.

"You've given up on your miracle."

Had he set aside the search for Mom's cure to help me, that would have been one thing. But this? Using my agenda as his suicide run? It wasn't an act of love. It was acceptance of her fate and his. That was all.

Lucky for him, I couldn't afford to care I was a last resort.

I had a cousin who needed all the help I could beg, borrow, or steal to free him.

"Be nice." Mom pinched my side, and I yelped. "That goes for both of you."

"I can be nice if he can." I made a little-girl pout. "Can you be nice, Daddy?"

A sigh moved through him that ended on a coarse laugh. "You truly are your mother's daughter."

"Now you're just trying to shift the blame onto me." Mom snorted. "Really, Saint. She's you in a wig."

"If you're done blaming each other for my shortcomings—" I wobbled a step, "—I need to go."

"*We.*" Mom crossed her arms over her chest. "We're coming with you." She stared at Dad. "Aren't *we*?"

"Yes, love." His eyes gentled, and so did his tone. "We're going with her."

"Excellent." She rubbed her hands together. "Where, exactly, are we going?"

"I have a rental." I gestured vaguely toward the former welcome center. "I can explain on the way."

"We'll follow from above," Dad countered with a haughty sniff. "I despise modern transportation."

"All right." I walked into the soupy water. "I would join you if I didn't have to return this car."

It was going to be a lonely trip back without Aedan, and I wasn't looking forward to how much thinking I could do in the quiet. A radio could drown out a person, but it couldn't muffle your thoughts.

"Leave it then." Dad dismissed it as being of no consequence. "I would love to see you fly."

"It's not so much flying as not falling." I felt an answering smile form, a reminder of how much I once longed for his approval. "Sadly, cars are expensive. I can't afford to buy the rental agency a new ride to replace this one if I ditch it."

One phone call, and I could task a local Black Hat with picking it up and returning it, but that would make them wonder what the deputy director was doing at a burned-down pit stop in the middle of nowhere. If they were ambitious enough to find out, their curiosity would bite me on the butt.

Even if I dialed the rental desk with the location for a pickup, I would be leaving a paper trail right back to the Devlin Wildlife Center.

Do that, and I might as well email the director and warn him Calixta was coming for him myself.

"Very well." He summoned his wings on a carrion breeze. "Perhaps later then?"

"Perhaps," I agreed, fighting another smile, and selected a souvenir spur of the moment before wading to my rental.

WORSE THAN CALLING THE RENTAL AGENCY AND EXPLAINING MY PLANS had changed, that I would turn the car in at a location closer to Samford, was the knowledge I was in for a ten-hour drive. Alone. With nothing but my guilt for company.

And maybe a golem.

But it would have been hard to escort my parents with a couple hundred tons of aluminum between us.

As soon as I was on the road, I paired my phone via Bluetooth to the car and dialed my best friend to break the news.

"About time," Clay growled at me. "I picked a bald spot on my wig waiting on you to call."

"Maybe you'll start a trend?" I ignored the faint tremble of my bottom lip. "The Return of Friar Tuck?"

I made the mistake of buying him a wig for his birthday six months into our partnership. It was cheap, but he wore it every day for a month. Until he was left with a bald crown and a fringe of synthetic hair.

Hence the nickname Friar Tuck.

Unwilling to be distracted, he bulled on. "What took you so long?"

A fist of emotion caught me by the throat, and I wished feelings didn't hit harder than physical blows.

"Aedan..." I tried to swallow, failed, then tried a second time. "He's gone, Clay."

The story spilled out of me in fits and starts, infuriating me when my voice refused to work or my hands trembled on the wheel or my eyes watered so hard I couldn't see through the windshield.

"Dollface," he said gently, after I was done. "He decided to be your Plan B before you left."

Certain I misheard him, I quit sniffling. "What?"

"Calixta was bound to view you as a liar and a betrayer. Aedan worried, in light of your last meeting, she wouldn't trust you to keep your word, even with a contract." He fell silent. "He left here prepared to offer himself in exchange, if she required further convincing."

"Why didn't you tell me?" I screamed at the phone. "I could have stopped this from happening."

Why did you let him leave? Why did you do this? Why did you give him up so easily?

The darkest parts of me wanted to pounce on this new information and use it to exonerate myself, but I knew better. This wasn't Clay's fault. It was mine.

"He didn't want you stuck choosing between him and Ace."

"Only because he was afraid I wouldn't have picked him."

"You're in fascination with Asa." He laid it out plain. "You would have chosen him."

I would rather stare at the sun until my eyes gave out than look within me to determine if he was right.

Now it was my turn to be frank. "We're getting him back."

A moment lapsed while he decided the best way to juggle that grenade without blowing off his hands. "How?"

"Dad and Mom showed up after the wards dissolved." I glanced at the roof like I might somehow glimpse them above me and realized I still didn't believe they were going to stay and help. I didn't fully trust them to be up there if I looked for them. "He thinks Calixta will trade. For the director."

"That's a big gamble," he said at last, "but we've had worse odds."

The war drum pounding in my chest, ready to storm the gates and drag the director out of his sanctuary by his hair, slowed a beat. "I know."

It wasn't a lie. I had known. I just hadn't let myself dwell on what would happen if this didn't work.

Like I hadn't dwelled on what I ought to be asking rather than gnawing my bottom lip bloody.

A bigger question loomed, *the* question, and I was terrified of his answer.

I wasn't sure I could put my fears into words without choking on them.

"Pull over." He issued the order with gentleness that made my stomach twist and knot. "I don't want you driving while we have this conversation."

Please be good news. Please be good news. Please be good news.

Hands trembling on the wheel, I cut onto the shoulder of the road and put the car in park. "Ready."

Ready? Ha! That was a good one. I wasn't sure I would ever be prepared to hear what he had to say.

"Ace is awake." A world of compassion filled his announcement. "He's asking to see you."

Tears burst from my eyes, sluicing down my cheeks, and my neck wilted until my forehead hit the wheel.

I tried to breathe, I did, but an iron band cinched around my chest. My heart. My lungs. My entire being vibrated with a relief so primal, I couldn't hold myself together any longer. I was falling apart. Crumbling. Shattering. I hiccupped snotty noises while every facial orifice leaked hot fluids that dripped off my chin.

"Shh," Clay soothed. "He's okay, Dollface."

As much as I wanted details, I couldn't move except to suck in air to fuel my gulping cries.

"Thanks to you and Aedan," he continued, "he's going to stay that way."

A loud bang on my window shocked me upright, but I had to wipe my eyes on my shirt to see out.

Expecting a concerned motorist or maybe a state trooper, I was stunned to find Dad standing there.

I had forgotten about him.

He pointed a finger at the door, and I unlocked it, allowing him to pull it open. He mashed the release on my seat belt then knelt on the wet grass and folded me into his arms. I clung to him as he stroked my hair and back with choppy motions that exposed how out of practice he was at comforting others.

"Here." He withdrew and offered me a white handkerchief that smelled like his magic. "Good news?"

Without knowing how long he'd stood there, wavering on whether to interfere or let me cry it out alone, I couldn't tell if he had overheard Clay and was being polite or if he really didn't know. Suddenly, it didn't matter.

"Yeah," I croaked, my throat raw. "Asa is awake." I flung myself back into Dad's arms. "I wasn't sure…"

"I know." He rubbed halting circles on my upper back. "I know."

"I understand why you did what you did. The animus vow." I skirted as close to forgiveness as I was likely to get for his betrayals. "You didn't think. You just felt. And the pain was so big, you couldn't hold it all in. You reacted to make it stop." I felt bad about the wet stain on his nice shirt. "I get that now."

"Perhaps you ought to check in with your friend," Dad suggested. "I doubt my presence is a comfort."

"Sorry I disappeared on you, Clay." I lifted my shirttail to wipe my face clean then remembered it was a soggy mess drying in sticky patches to my skin and searched for the handkerchief I must have dropped. "Dad's here."

With his hearing, Clay probably already knew, but I figured it was polite to tell him we had company.

"I'll let you go then." He hesitated. "Call me if you want company."

"I will," I promised before hitting the end button.

"He's your anchor." Dad helped me get straight in my seat before clarifying. "Clay, I mean."

"He's my best friend." I wasn't sure I had ever told him that in seriousness. "He's like a brother to me."

A warning edge trimmed my tone in case Dad had opinions on who I spent my time with these days.

"If I'd had a friend like that, maybe I wouldn't have made the same choices."

It was as close to an apology as I was likely to get from him, and it was more than I had ever hoped for.

This didn't fix everything, it didn't repair us, but it patched things up enough I could let him go. I could breathe again. I could steady myself. I could…glare at Mom who waited several feet away with tears in her eyes over the scene she had no doubt orchestrated and kept her distance to avoid interrupting.

"We should get moving." I elected not to ruin the moment. "I'm steady now."

"All right." Dad eyed me until he made his own decision. "We'll be right above you if you need us."

The warmth spreading through my chest I blamed on my already heightened emotions. I couldn't afford to get used to being Daddy's little girl. It hurt too much when he inevitably reminded me where his true loyalties lay. But still. It was nice. I decided to enjoy it while I had it and not beat myself up over it later.

Once they were airborne, I got back on the road leading to Alabama.

Five miles later, the phone rang again.

"What's the number one rule?" Colby's chastisement filled the car. *"Call the second you're safe."*

"I did call."

"You didn't call *me*." She growled a mothy growl. "So it doesn't count."

"You're right." I wiped my nose on my sleeve to avoid tipping her off about my crying jag. "I'm terrible."

"That's right," she urged me on. "If you were a member of my crew, you'd be walking the plank."

Her stern mood told me Clay hadn't prepared her for Aedan not coming back, and I didn't have the heart to break hers over the phone. I wanted to look her in the eye when I told her what Aedan had done, for all of us.

"How's Peleg?" I angled for a new topic before my throat closed again. "Are you still reading to him?"

"He's unconscious, but he's mumbling and twitching in his sleep. The doctor said that's a good sign."

"That's great." I was glad to hear it. "Maybe when he wakes up you can indoctrinate him into your cult."

"How many times do I have to tell you?" She heaved a sigh up all the way from her toes. "It's a *guild*."

"Mmm-hmm."

"I saw Asa." Her voice came out small, timid. "He let me braid his hair to keep it away from the doctors."

Good thing Clay had been there for treatment, otherwise that might have ended poorly for them.

Not much of a market for surgeons without hands.

"That was nice of you." I felt a smile creep up on me. "I hope you took pictures."

"I put my blanket on him too. I know it's not supposed to work for anyone else, but…I wanted to help."

"Just being there will work wonders." I blinked away my fuzzy vision. "Have you seen Blay?"

"No." She didn't sound happy about it either. "The doctor said we might not for a while."

Between the two of them, Asa was the more docile patient, but I worried how Blay was doing.

Physically, he would heal alongside Asa.

Emotionally, he deserved to know it wasn't only Asa we were

waiting on to wake.

"When I get back, we'll see what we can do to speed things along." I hardened my determination. "We've healed him before. Now that the doctors have done the heavy lifting, I bet we can help Asa purge the remnants of cold iron from his system. As soon as Asa is at one hundred percent, he should be able to safely shift again."

"I'll go eat so I'm ready when you get here."

"You haven't been skipping meals, have you?"

"Only lunch. Maybe dinner?" She explained, "Clay needed my help saving his ship from pirates."

"From pirates?" I glanced down at my phone. "Aren't you guys the pirates?"

"Rue." She paused for dramatic effect. "We're *privateers.*"

I must have missed a memo somewhere. "What's the difference?"

"We've gone legit. We only pirate the pirates now. For the queen." She scoffed. "*Huge* difference."

"Forgive my ignorance," I apologized solemnly. "I didn't mean to imply you were lowly scallywags."

"There are more rules," she lamented, "but also more loot."

Happy to let her distract me, I settled in for a lecture on the history of reformed pirates and her plans to train messenger pigeons. They would fly between her guildmates' ships to keep them apprised of current goings-on without using the language of flags, which enemies could learn and use against them.

Just last month one ship misread a flag and fired on another, which returned fire. Rinse and repeat. The result was a sunken ship, twenty dead, and two guildmates who didn't speak to each other for a week.

Short of sticking a crewman in a boat to play mailman, she felt pigeons were the best option.

And, though I was hardly qualified to offer my advice, I agreed they were a solid investment.

Too bad *investment* ended with me opening my wallet to provide seed money for her new enterprise.

Me and my big mouth.

CHAPTER EIGHTEEN

*G*iven Dad's reputation as a notoriously cruel black witch of legendary power, and Mom's iffy status as a vengeful spirit, I couldn't roll up to the farm in good conscience without first consulting its residents. Not after the Peleg incident. I couldn't afford to give the centuria, or Moran, any reason to distrust me or my motives if I wanted Colby to remain safe while she was within the boundaries of the farm.

At the edge of the ward, I parked and let Moran and Clay come investigate.

As soon as I stepped out of the car, Dad landed next to me, and Mom slid to the ground beside him.

Within minutes, Clay roared up on a beefy four-wheeler that must be new, kicking up plumes of dirt.

Above him, Moran glided, waiting for Clay to hit the brakes before touching down beside him.

"What's the holdup?" He revved the engine. "If you don't get your butt to the infirmary, Ace will flop out of bed and inchworm his way down the driveway. Which, now that I'm picturing it, would be *hilarious.*"

Eager as I was to see Asa, to touch him, to reassure myself, I had to hold strong. "We need to talk first."

"Okay." He turned off the four-wheeler. "What's up?"

"Moran, these are my parents." I indicated Dad and then Mom. "Hiram and Vonda Nádasdy." I gestured to her for their benefit. "This is Primipilus Moran."

"A pleasure." Moran placed her hand over her heart. "Your daughter is a remarkable woman."

"Yes," Dad said, his eyes on me. "She is."

A flush heated my nape at the praise, and Clay cocked an eyebrow when I didn't snap out a retort.

Probably something along the lines of *no thanks to you.*

"You're in charge?" Mom tucked herself against Dad's side. "This place is lovely."

"Yes," I answered for Moran. "Moran and her centuria are here to protect Samford in the coming days."

"The town and its people are dear to Rue." Mom touched her throat. "Thank you for your service."

A pleased smile spread across Moran's face that tightened to concern when she turned to me. "Why the formality, Princess?"

Mom elbowed Dad in the side, amused to have birthed a princess.

Former princess.

"There have been...developments." I invited them outside the wards then cast a privacy spell around us. "I felt you ought to have a say in how the next few minutes unfold, Moran, since these are your people."

Her eyes widened on me. "Princess?"

"Calixta Damaris will soon claim the high throne of Hael." There was no way to soften that blow and no doubt in my mind that she would win. A woman scorned and all that. "I won't be a future princess for much longer." I wasn't sure how this next bit would affect her, and the centuria, but we had to figure that part out too. "I assume you've all seen the broadcast?"

"Yeah." Clay rubbed his jaw. "I secured the footage for them."

"Then you know Asa has been disinherited."

Rules were rules. Clay made that clear on my first visit to the arena. Even then, I nearly broke them.

This time, I had shattered them to itty-bitty pieces by saving Blay.

"Yes," she said slowly, with a trace of worry. "Has the former high queen formalized your status?"

"As persona non grata?" I wanted to vomit as I admitted, "She named Aedan as her heir."

"I thought…" Moran let that line of inquiry die. "Will you be safe from her?"

"We have a contract, which will provide Asa and me with broad protection from her, but we must remain vigilant until she's settled on her throne." I indicated my folks. "They're going to help me get Aedan back once the dust clears."

"All right." Her gaze touched on Clay. "I still don't understand the formality."

"I want you to have a say." I jerked my chin toward the farm. "Before my parents cross the wards."

Poor Moran's eyes almost bugged out of her head. *"Me?"*

"The centuria are your people. You deserve to make the call if you want my folks mingling with them."

"I…" Her daze made it easy to tell how little control she'd had over her life. "I trust your judgment."

"You might want to hold off on that." I banished the privacy spell then gestured for everyone else to wait for us. "There's one more matter I want to discuss with you." I waved for her to follow. "In private."

Once we had distanced ourselves, I set another spell then reinforced it and kept our backs to the others to avoid any pesky lip-reading attempts.

As much as I didn't want to have this conversation, I was as volatile as ever. So was Colby. For those reasons, I owed Moran an explanation of what happened to her son if I ever wanted to begin mending the rift this incident had torn between us.

Failing that, if we parted as enemies, at least I could trust her to come at my front and not at my back.

Slowly, I began explaining about The Hunk in loose terms. I told her why Clay didn't know all the specifics, exonerating him from not telling her, and why the more knowledge he held, the greater potential threat he posed to anyone caught in the director's crosshairs.

"Colby did that to Peleg?" Moran's wings twitched against her back. "Could she do it again?"

There was no point in lying. "Yes, and yes."

"She wouldn't have hurt him like that of her own accord," Moran allowed, "but it worries me what else she might do." She paused. "Children often react before they think, and her reaction was...catastrophic."

As loudly as the voice in my head begged to point out her son wouldn't have gotten harmed if he kept his hands to himself, she was right that kids tended to follow knee-jerk instincts, but Colby's were now lethal. "Yes."

"That makes you a threat too."

"Yes."

"If I asked you both to leave until this matter was under control, would you go?"

Prepared for this possibility, I simply nodded. "I'm willing to relocate us for the time being."

That was the great thing about houses on wheels. The freedom to move them when the need arose.

"All right." She stepped back. "Do you think your parents would prefer a bunk or tent?"

Oops.

That fast, I forgot I had to provide guest accommodations.

In my defense, Mom and Dad never stuck around long enough to need a place to stay.

"They can use our tiny house," I decided, since it would give them privacy.

For things I didn't want to think about.

Ever.

"Four people won't fit in there."

"With Colby and me gone, they'll have plenty of room. That frees up two houses."

Until Asa was cleared by his doctors, he could keep his butt right here where it was safe.

I could negotiate visitation hours until then, if that was what it took to make her comfortable.

"I'm not evicting either of you." She looked at me like I was crazy. "I wouldn't do that to you or Colby."

"I'm confused." I massaged my temples. "You said we were threats. I agreed. I thought that was that?"

"We're all threats in one way or another. That's not the problem." She picked at her thumbnail, a sign of how uncomfortable having power, having a say, made her. "I'm not casting you out of the sanctuary you helped us build, but I would appreciate more honesty and to be apprised of all threats to our people."

"There will be times when I can't tell you everything, or that I must forbid you to share what you know."

"You mean with Clay." Her unhappiness with that verdict mirrored my own. "He's that big of a risk?"

"Honestly? I ought to cut him out of my life to protect Colby and all my other secrets. Especially now."

"Will you?"

"No." As if there was more than one possible answer. "He's family."

"You extend the same courtesies to others that you ask for yourself."

"I practice what I preach, if that's what you're asking."

The phrase threw her, if the crinkle of her brow was any indication, but she divined the meaning. "Yes."

While I understood the plan had always been to mold myself into a good person, a better version of me that Colby could be proud of, it always shocked me to discover other people believed the act I put on.

Fake it 'til you make it.

Go through the motions, always choose to do the least harm, and those habits became ingrained beliefs.

While I had her alone, I wanted to check. "Do you have any more questions for me?"

"No." She drew out the word. "Can I come to you if I think of more later?"

"Always."

"Rue?"

"Thought of something that fast?"

"I just…" She flung herself at me, enfolding me in her arms and within her wings. "Thank you." Hot tears hit my neck. "For setting me free. For giving me back my son. For giving us both a chance at a new life."

Awkwardly, I hugged her back. "You're welcome."

"We should get you to the infirmary before Asa comes looking for you."

On that happy note, I pivoted, ready to do that very thing, and my smile fell. "Oh crap."

In the main aisle of the barn—I mean, clinic—Asa leaned against the doorway with a hand pressed to his abdomen. Dr. Nadir trailed him, trying to urge him back to his room. I say *urge*, because Dr. Nadir had spotted me and decided putting hands on Asa was a bad idea. But that meant he kept right on coming for me.

When he took another step, and another, I cursed under my breath and dropped the barrier.

"Gotta go." I left Moran behind and jogged past Clay. "Keep my parents here." I reached Asa in strides. "Why are you out of bed?"

"I was worried about you." His voice whistled through his lungs. "You left."

"I did," I confirmed, tucking my shoulder under his arm. "We'll talk about it after you've rested, okay?"

"All I've done is rest." He groaned from the strain of standing. "Can we sit outside for a minute?"

Like magic, Clay appeared with a hay bale from the waiting room and set it behind Asa's knees. He must have followed us to make sure we didn't strip naked and put on a show for our guests.

As if we were that reckless.

I mean…

Okay.

We didn't have the best track record with PDA, but even we weren't *that* bad.

With a sigh of relief, Asa sat under the sun and sagged on his bones while I checked to ensure my parents were right where I left them until I had time to key the wards to them.

"A few minutes won't hurt him." Clay clipped my shoulder with his. "Stop babying him."

The narrowing of my eyes warned him I had a low threshold for shenanigans after the last few days.

"I can admit when I'm wrong." Clay stepped back then flicked his wrist. "Baby him all you want."

"I will." I knelt in front of Asa and captured his face between my palms. "How do you feel?"

"I've gained a new respect for beef tenderized with a mallet."

"Goddess." I rested my forehead in his lap. "I thought I lost you."

"You won't let that happen." He stroked my hair. "I believe that."

Behind us was living—and dead—proof it didn't matter how much you loved someone, or believed in them, they could still die and turn your world upside down. "You have more faith in me than I do."

"I received a messenger from Grandmother while you were away."

Heart rising in my throat, I had to swallow past the lump to get out the words. "What did she say?"

"She will continue her research on your condition, but she's exhausted her resources at the temple." He lightly scratched my scalp in a way that made me want to curl up across his thighs and purr. "Her only way forward is to travel to Faerie in the hopes the elders who taught her Tinkkit will have answers."

"It's not a solution, but it's not a dead end." I puffed out my cheeks on an exhale. "I'll take it."

"Your parents," he said, as if just noticing them. "Clay mentioned they're going to stay and help?"

"That's what they say today." I rubbed my cheek on his thigh. "Tomorrow, who knows?"

As far as missions went, ours dovetailed nicely.

Dad would get revenge on his father, albeit in a different manner than he intended.

That might or might not pacify Luca, I was betting on *not*, but I could fake optimism for a few hours.

Calixta wouldn't kill the director outright. She had suffered too much for too long at his hands to let him off that easy. What she did to him would be as ugly and as creative as what he had done to her.

If it got Aedan back, I didn't care if she skinned the director, stuffed him, and roasted him over an open fire.

And, with him out of the picture, that left Clay the next best thing to a free man.

"Saint has given up?" Asa raked his fingers through my hair. "He's actually going to let your mom go?"

"That's what she believes, but it's not in his nature to quit. He's plotting. I just don't know what yet."

"I'm inclined to agree." He made a thoughtful sound. "Do you think it's safe for him to be here?"

"Any scheme of his will be localized," I assured him. "He probably wants a peek at the grimoire."

There was no use in denying I possessed it. The best I could hope for was to keep it out of his hands.

"That's enough sunshine for you," Clay announced. "The doctors have cleared you to sleep in your own bed, but that's it. Sleep. No funny business." He singled me out next with an equally stern glare. "You better check in with Colby soon, or she'll name her next ship after you and sink it out of spite."

"I'm good here." Asa tipped his head back. "Rue, you can go check in with Colby."

"Nice try, but no cigar." Clay scooped Asa in his arms before he could protest. "Alley-oop."

"I knew I kept you around for a reason." I led the way to our house and opened the door. "After you."

Careful of his injuries, Clay laid Asa out on our bed but let me cover him and get him comfortable.

"I'll be fine," Asa murmured, eyes falling shut. "Go visit Colby."

Before I could decide what to do, he conked out in a dead sleep.

"You better get going." Clay chuckled when Asa's mouth dropped open. "Shorty isn't the forgiving sort."

With a gentle hand, he ushered me out and down the steps, but I couldn't get my feet to move.

"Ace had the right idea." He leaned against the door. "Pretty day." He squinted up at the bright-blue sky. "Might as well enjoy it." He noticed my eyes leaking and wiped my cheek dry. "None of that, Dollface."

Uncertain what I had done to deserve a friend like Clay, I considered hugging him again to hide my tears.

Feelings were dumb. So dumb. Emotions ruined everything.

"Rue." A blur of white smacked into my throat with the force of a punch. "You're back."

Gagging and coughing, I patted Colby's head while praying her enthusiasm hadn't crushed my trachea.

Thank the goddess I had been in too much of a hurry to reach Asa to let my parents onto the farm yet.

Ivana, eyes puffy and posture stiff, inclined her head to me but made no move to abandon her post.

No one could stay on duty around the clock without exhaustion impacting their ability to do their job.

Talking to her about the importance of taking time off, more than just switching out with Clay while she slept or ate, moved up my to-do list. I admired her dedication, but she was running on fumes.

"Can you get pre-bored?" Colby shoved my hand then smoothed her fluff. "I heard the news. About my upcoming incarceration. I'll get so tired of being locked up all day every day I already feel twitchy."

"You'll survive." I kissed the top of her fuzzy head. "How about we move Clay in with you?"

I slid him a glance to make sure he was okay with the plans I was making up as I went along.

"Really?" She restyled her fuzz then turned to Clay. "You would do that?"

No surprise, a devilish light entered his eyes at the idea of unsupervised 24/7 mischief.

"Shorty," he said earnestly, "I would pay good money to hang out with you all day every day."

Wings fluttering with happiness, she ditched me and sailed over to his shoulder.

"My parents can sleep in your house, Clay." I scanned for them. "That way, we can keep an eye on Dad."

"That's mighty close to Colby." Clay pointed to the roof. "What about the connecting tubes?"

"We'll disconnect those." I added it to my to-do list. "I'll also set new wards around her house."

"That will draw your father's attention like a magnet," he warned. "He'll know you're hiding something."

"He'll think that's where I'm stashing the grimoire," I realized. "Okay, so, new plan."

For him to bust in and discover Colby would be ten times worse than him locating the grimoire.

"No wards?" Colby's suggestion wasn't a bad one. "I have plenty of exits, and I'll have Clay."

"I don't like this." I rubbed my face. "I don't expect my parents to stick around long, but Dad could cause major trouble for us while he's here."

"There's another option, but you might not like it." Clay pursed his lips. "They could stay at your home."

Home.

Minus the safe full of dark artifacts residing in my closet, I could get behind that idea.

There truly was no good place to stash my parents that didn't involve the potential for disaster.

"How rude would it be if I booked them a room outside of town?" I joked. Sort of. "Scale of one to ten."

"That kind of distance will only convince your father you're hiding things from him."

"But she *is* hiding things from him," Colby argued the point. "Won't he already expect that?"

The conversation shook something loose, an idea. "Maybe we should lean into that."

"What are you thinking?" Clay, as usual, looked ready for anything. "Warding ant hills to throw him off the scent? We have a million, and it would serve him right for snooping if they—"

A dull thump, the sound of a body hitting the floor, shot my heart into my throat and sent me sprinting up the steps into the house.

CHAPTER NINETEEN

"*B*athroom," Asa explained from flat on his back, one hand curving protectively around his stomach.

"You could have asked for help." I knelt beside him. "We were right outside the door."

With his super hearing, he must have heard us bumping our gums for the last ten minutes.

"Hmm." A twitch moved through his lips. "Would you have asked for help?"

Clay turned his chuckle into a cough that no one believed then leaned against the wall to give us room.

"That's not the point." I checked him over to make sure he hadn't pulled his stitches. "Colby and I were going to boost your healing after you rested, but I see you can't be trusted to behave." She leapt onto my shoulder, but tremors ran through her legs. "You ready, Captain?"

"What if...?" She buried her face against my neck. "I didn't mean to hurt Peleg, but..."

"You're not going to hurt me." Asa sounded certain beyond any doubt. "What happened with Peleg was an accident. You were alone and scared then. Rue is here now. She'll guide you through it." He reached out to stroke her downy spine. "But only if you want to try."

If I didn't already love him beyond reason, beyond sanity, I would have fallen for him then. He had a way of encouraging her to be brave while always reassuring her we were here to catch her. She could try and fail then try again and fail again. He made sure she never worried we would hold her choices against her.

"I'll try." She fluffed herself to maximum poof. "I can do this."

"You can do anything you put your mind to," I assured her, knowing as well as he did that the longer she shied away from her magic, the less control she would have when it came time to use it. "But Asa is right. You don't *have* to do this. It's your call. If you're not ready, then you're not ready. I can manage it solo."

"No." She flexed her wings. "I have to get stronger than The Hunk, right?"

Until Naeema returned from her research trip, we had to learn how to control the magic. Or it would control us. "We both do."

As much as I hated to admit it—to think it—Dad was a good how-to resource.

But he was also a lethal one made deadlier if I granted him access, even for educational purposes.

"Rue?" Clay leaned forward. "You okay?"

"Yeah. Sorry." Palms on Asa's abdomen, I focused where Stavros almost disemboweled him. "Ready."

Warmth spread from Colby's feet onto my shoulder. It flowed down my arms, mingling with the magic in my hands, and melding into soothing heat that mended the damage under Asa's skin. As that healed, I turned our focus toward purging the cold iron from his system. Leaving it there wasn't an option. It would undo all the work we had just done, reinfecting him, and weakening him all over again.

She and I were so perfectly in sync, I didn't notice her light battling dark whirls of my magic to reach him at first. The second I understood, I jerked back, severing the connection, hating the whiff of rot in the air.

"The grimoire tainted your magic." Asa caught my hand and held it. "It didn't taint you."

"You feel the same to me." Colby rested her forehead against me.

"There's resistance between us, like a sheet of paper, but I can punch through it. On the other side, that's when it gets murky. Like before."

Before she was my familiar and her magic ran through my veins, cleansing the rot in my soul.

"Colby." Asa angled his head toward her. "Could you purge Rue?"

The twining of our magics cleansed me, that much we had established, but I couldn't afford to waste her strength when it was needed elsewhere.

"A little black magic in my system won't hurt me." I brought his hand to my mouth and kissed his knuckles. "I was a black witch for most of my life. A brief return to my roots won't kill me."

As long as I kept my teeth to myself and avoided the lure of juicy, pulsating meat, I could rebound.

"Listen to her, Ace." Clay threw his weight in with mine. "She knows what she can handle."

Oh to have as much faith in myself as he had in me.

"All right." Asa held out his hand for Colby to light on his palm. "Just don't drain yourself on my behalf."

Scrunching her face in concentration, she pushed her light down his arm and into his chest until his torso illuminated from within. Droplets of viscous silver-black liquid squeezed out his pores and ran in rivulets down his sides to pool on the floor in mercurial swirls.

Three minutes in, she trembled, only once, and Asa ended the session by placing her on the floor.

"Well?" I picked her up, cradled her against my chest, then turned to him. "How do you feel?"

Asa inhaled, expanding his lungs fully, then exhaled past his lips. "Like a million doubloons."

"A million doubloons," Colby said dreamily. "Can you even imagine?"

"Come on." I offered him a hand up before he got too comfy. "Let's put you back in bed, so I can get my parents settled for the night."

Steady on his feet, for the most part, he cleared his throat and jerked his chin toward the bathroom.

"New plan." I set Colby on the bed then hooked my arm through his. "Potty break and then bed."

"Potty break." Clay dissolved into laughter. "Does the wittle prince need to tinkle?"

Giggling like a loon, Colby flew over to The Bad Influence while I escorted Asa to the bathroom.

"Sorry about that." I shut us in together. "I should have known not to tempt children with potty humor."

"I heard that," Clay yelled from his spot near the door, then burst into song, "Tinkle, tinkle, little prince…"

If I smiled, and I'm not saying I did, I hid it well, seeing as how I was facing the door to give Asa privacy.

"Are you sure you can't live without him?" Asa handled his business, washed his hands, then came up behind me and rested his chin on my shoulder. "How about another decade apart?"

"Tempting." I had to admit, he might be onto something. "Very tempting."

"Don't worry," Colby reassured Clay. "I would still play Mystic Realms with you long distance."

"You just don't want to lose a captain in your fleet," Clay grumbled. "Where's the love?"

"I *do* love you, but how can I become an admiral without competent staff? Have you seen Aedan play?"

The mention of Aedan crushed my lungs until I had to remind myself to breathe.

"Staff." Clay gasped. *"Staff?"* I pictured him pinning his wrist to his forehead. "How dare you?"

Their altercation dissolved into a fit of screams, giggles, and yelps before cutting off with a slam.

Glancing over my shoulder, I raised an eyebrow. "Think it's safe?"

"As it ever is around here." He reached around me to open the door. "Let's investigate."

Sure enough, Clay had taken Colby back to her house, no doubt to log on and begin their privateering.

"The coast is clear," I announced. "That means you're going to bed, mister."

After climbing into his spot, he patted the mattress with a contented sigh. "Join me?"

"Don't mind if I do." I ought to be playing host to my parents, but I wanted to breathe Asa in and let the knowledge he was well and whole settle before I left him again. "I can spare a few moments of my time, I guess, since you did almost die to get my attention."

"Yes," he said dryly. "That's why Blay challenged my father. To get your attention."

"Flashy." I lifted a shoulder. "He could have bought me cupcakes, like you did."

"Hmm."

He caressed my wrist, his fingers warm and sure, and fastened on a new bracelet woven from his hair.

"Asa…" More tears threatened, but I must have hit my quota for the day. "It's beautiful."

This design was more intricate than the one before, a true work of art, and it made me feel…whole.

A faint blush threatened his cheeks when he saw how moved I was by the gesture. "It's nothing."

"Don't do that." With it on, I felt more myself than I had in days. "Don't make it less." I resisted the urge to hug it to myself. "You're a gifted craftsman, and I love your work. Thank you. Really. Thanks."

"I did it for selfish reasons," he confessed. "I want everyone to know you're mine."

"Have we ruled out the forehead tattoos? I can't remember if those got a thumbs-up or thumbs-down."

"I'm game if you are." His eyelids slipped lower. "I won't even make you glamour me to hide it."

"That would defeat the purpose anyway." I collapsed beside him, hooked my thigh over his, and latched my arm across his chest. I rested my head on his shoulder and my nose at his throat. I was as cuddled up to him as I could get without burrowing under his skin. "This has been a *looong* week. I need a vacation."

An offer to sweep me off my feet was what I expected, but what I got instead was a soft snore.

With the pain no longer ravaging Asa, his body had decided to shut down and rest. I couldn't blame him, but I also couldn't justify lying in bed with my brain buzzing like a hive of bees, not when I had yet to settle my parents in. Kind of rude to leave them on the border with Moran babysitting them.

There was also a bargain that needed striking away from curious ears.

There was no time to contact Meg again, but I didn't need an iron-clad contract for this deal.

After padding into the bathroom, I shut the door and set a privacy spell before dialing Marita. "Hey."

The souvenir I took from the swamp jabbed me in the hip when I leaned against the sink, and I withdrew a twisted length of red cypress that would become my new wand. The tree had been drinking water rich with Calixta's victims for decades. I couldn't think of a more fitting conduit for my corrosive magic.

"Hold on." She covered the speaker then shouted in the background. "Rue's on the phone."

"Do I need to put on pants?" Derry yelled back. "I can be ready for adventure in five seconds flat."

"You heard the man." She returned her attention to me. "He's got his adventure pants ready."

"I'm not sure this qualifies as an adventure." I swallowed a laugh. "He can still wear the pants, though. If he's dead set on it."

"Oh?" A door shut. Probably between her and Derry. "What do you have in mind?"

To her credit, she didn't sound any less enthusiastic.

Clearly, she believed I was an agent of chaos.

To be fair, I kind of was.

"I have a collection of dark magic artifacts I need to relocate and secure."

"The mausoleum stash?"

Whoever had sponsored the Boo Brothers' decades-long crusade against paranormals had armed them with arcane relics aplenty. Now their entire collection was mine, and I had accrued more deadly trinkets than ever.

"Plus a few more pieces," I hedged. "Very dangerous pieces."

"Of course."

"Meg told me once that you guys have a storage building empire with complimentary security."

"One of our more lucrative side hustles," she agreed. "It started out as a passion project for Derry's dad, who's a packrat and needed a place to hide his junk from his mate. We were shocked, her most of all, when it exploded into a dependable revenue stream. Turns out plenty of other wargs have crap a mate would love to watch burn." She groaned. "Don't even get me started on the vampires. The useless garbage they amass over a lifetime is *ridiculous*. There's one guy who collects ramen noodles. *Why?* He can't even eat them."

"Seems like if you corner the vampire market, you guys would be set for life."

"We're big believers in the *don't put all your eggs in one basket* approach to wealth management, but it wouldn't hurt my feelings if humoring undead hoarders doubled the pack's income."

"If I ever manage to amass any wealth, I'll be sure to ask for your two cents on how to grow it."

Aside from my assortment of three-fund portfolios, each under a different alias, I wasn't doing as much to build a nest egg as I could.

I had spent so much of my money running, and then building a life, I hadn't recovered from the financial hits before Black Hat scooped me up again. Now I had more disposable income and could get creative with my write-offs, but I didn't want to be spinning in this hamster wheel forever. I was young for a witch with my life expectancy, but I ought to sit down with Clay and let him coach me on how to make Colby and me financially secure.

The man had more money than Croesus, and he didn't mind sharing the wealth of his knowledge.

"We're happy to accept your business, but are you sure you want your objects inventoried? We keep a thorough accounting of property in those locations. You wouldn't believe how degraded memory gets with the long-lived races. They'll swear up and down they left an item they've lost in our care, and if we don't have records to back us up, we're liable. The records are sealed, of course, but with a client like you, we couldn't guarantee anonymity."

"Are you saying I'm a troublemaker?"

"More like a high-value target with lots of high-value trinkets and high-risk enemies."

Meaning I put the others' possessions at risk if anyone discovered I had a locker there.

"Fair." I rested my hip against the sink. "Are you turning down my application?"

"More like suggesting you apply to a specialized sector. More Fort Knox and less Store 'N Save."

"Does Fort Knox leave a paper trail?"

"It leaves no trail." She sounded gleeful. "Whatsoever."

Interesting. "How does it work?"

"We send you a box. You put things in the box. You seal the box. We take the box. We hide the box."

Even more interesting. "How do I access the box, if the need arises?"

"There's the rub. This service is recommended for clients who want their goods locked up and the key as good as thrown away. Clients approved for the program must be willing to live without their deposits for a decade or more. Nervous Nellies need not apply. This is a long-term storage solution. Emphasis on the *long*. The best way to keep the location private, and the boxes safe, is to avoid frequent contact."

This was sounding better and better. "How does the box get to me?"

"That's the best part." She howled with laughter. "We poached a gwyllgi from a pack out of Atlanta. The sucker mated in. Trust me, he already regrets his life choices. Not his mate, but his mate's kin. Poor man had no idea what he was getting into, and she didn't tell him for that exact reason. He handles those pickups."

A gwyllgi.

That was easily the most interesting tidbit yet. You didn't find that type of fae this side of Faerie often. "And where does he drop off?"

"A pocket realm." Her voice turned sly. "That's all you get."

A pocket realm could be anchored anywhere. No one would find it unless they knew where to look.

"Does everyone have their own pocket realm these days?"

"Only the cool kids." I heard a shrug in her voice. "We were given this one in lieu of payment. It remained stable for a year, so we had some witches come in and spruce things up a bit. Fortify the structure of the spells. Make sure it wouldn't disappear on us. We decided to use it as an offshoot of my father-in-law's business to keep him from filling the thing to the top with crap." She paused. "Though I could have won major bonus points with my mother-in-law if I let him dump his lifetime's accumulation in there then cut it loose." She sighed. "Ah well. My missed opportunity is your potential solution."

"Put me on the books for a pickup then." I braced myself for the strength to say what came next. "Don't tell me what it costs or how often it renews. You have my bank info. Take what you need to set me up."

"You really do like to live dangerously, huh?"

"On the knife's edge."

"I'll be in touch to arrange a time and place for the pickup." A husky note entered her voice. "Until then, Derry has no pants on, adventure or otherwise. He looks cold and—"

"Do *not* tell Rue I turtled," he bellowed in the background. "I'm as erect as the Eiffel Tower—"

"Let's not start comparing your dong to architectural feats, unless we're talking the gift shop edition."

A roar rattled my eardrums seconds before the call ended on her wild laughter.

With that done, I relaxed into the momentary quiet then dissolved the spell and crept outside.

Unsettled as it left me to walk away from Asa, he was in good shape thanks to Colby.

And I owed someone else a visit.

Maybe even an apology.

CHAPTER TWENTY

*P*urple face, split lip, swollen eyes, and a cut from her jaw to her clavicle.

Callula had definitely seen better days.

"Hi." I invited myself in, uncertain she would do the same if I asked first. "Good to see you're awake."

"I liked it better when I was asleep," she said cautiously. "How is my son?"

"I purged the cold iron from his system." I twiddled my thumbs. "He'll heal now."

Most of the credit belonged to Colby, but I wasn't ready to have that conversation with her yet.

"Good." An exhalation parted her lips that cost her a groan of pain. "Thank you."

"I'm sure you heard the news that Dvorak is dead. I wish I could have made him suffer, but he didn't."

"He's dead." She brought a hand to her lip, touching the scabbed corner. "That's what matters."

"Yes." I drummed my fingers on my knee and got to the point. "Stavros will be dead soon too."

"Stavros has no heir, and Asa has been renounced." Her frown deepened. "Who will inherit the throne?"

"Fun fact." I wiped my palms on my jeans. "Calixta Damaris is my grandmother."

The color washed out of her face, leaving it stark white with grayish blotches.

"I struck a bargain with her." I saw no need to get into specifics. "She's going to challenge Stavros."

A spark of something lit her eyes. "Will that make you her heir?"

"No." I had to clear my throat to find my voice. "She has chosen my cousin, Aedan, as her successor."

"Then you're free." She sat up until the pain hit too hard, and she slumped back. "Both of you."

"That's the plan." I tried yet again to quit fidgeting. "We'll know soon enough if it worked out."

As soon as Calixta wiped the floor with Stavros, *everyone* would know.

"I shouldn't have treated you," she said slowly, feeling out the words, "as I did on our first meeting."

The way she looked at me, like she had never seen me before, or maybe not so clearly, unsettled me.

"We don't have to have this conversation now." I stuck my hands in my pockets. "You should rest."

"You're not the daughter-in-law I envisioned, but you are the mate he needs. I see that now. I wish I had understood it sooner." She sank back against her pillows. "Do you think we can start again?"

"Depends." I squinted at the IV threading her hand. "Are you serious, or is this the drugs talking?"

"Perhaps a little of both?" A soft laugh escaped her, causing her to wince. "Take the win, Rue."

"Here's to new beginnings." I shook her hand to seal the deal. "Do you need anything?"

"More drugs." She let her eyes slide closed. "More sleep."

"I'll leave you to rest then." I backed toward the door. "I'll pass your request along to Dr. Nadir."

Pretty sure she was out cold by the time I crossed the threshold, but I sent the doctor in anyway.

On my way back to Asa, I received the call I had been dreading, and I had no choice but to answer.

"You have yet to return to work," the director snarled in my ear. "Rumors are circulating that Hiram was spotted in the French Quarter." He let the ensuing silence build. "Did you see him? Talk to him? Did you learn what he's planning? Why he's in New Orleans?"

No more pretense. No more games. No more hiding.

He knew that I knew Dad was alive, and the quaver in his voice perked my ears, a predator sighting prey.

And I was reminded that the boogieman of my childhood was simply a scared old man too afraid of the consequences of his actions to step out from behind his high walls and locked gates. He wanted power, glory, perhaps immortality, but he didn't want to pay for them out of his own hide.

He had always been a spider poised on an intricate web of his own design, but the sticky strands intended to trap his prey had snared him too. He was a prisoner to his vast network of spies, his paranoia, his fears.

I quit.

That was what I wanted to shout until my throat bled or his eardrums burst.

I was done with the lies and subterfuge. I was done being a weapon instead of a person. I was done with everyone I loved paying their pound of flesh to stand with me. I was just done.

But I had to suck it up and endure a while longer. I couldn't afford to lose access to the director.

Because one day, I would walk in through the front door, down the hall, and invite myself into his office. I would zap him with so much power that smoke curled out of his ears, spellbind his deadly hands and lying mouth, break his wand over my knee, then march him out to an SUV waiting to ferry him to whatever eternal damnation Calixta had devised for him. And *then* I would go get my cousin back.

The days had blurred into one endless smudge of time since we returned from New Orleans.

Had that been three real-time days ago. No. Four? Um. Maybe five?

Not that an exact number mattered this far past what he would view as an excusable work absence.

Which meant I needed a juicy tidbit I could fling into his mouth upon entering his office before his jaws snap closed around me. Good thing I had the perfect morsel to sacrifice on the altar of self-preservation.

An insurrectionist who rallied rogue witches against Black Hat.

A double agent who set his prize prisoner free after infiltrating the Bureau under his nose.

A schemer who traded my dad his freedom in exchange for the director's life.

Yes.

Luca fit the bill, and it was past time she paid for her betrayals.

Especially if it bought me an extension on when mine came due.

ABOUT THE AUTHOR

USA Today best-selling author Hailey Edwards writes about questionable applications of otherwise perfectly good magic, the transformative power of love, the family you choose for yourself, and blowing stuff up. Not necessarily all at once. That could get messy.

www.HaileyEdwards.net

ALSO BY HAILEY EDWARDS

Fish Out of Water

Lorimar Pack Series

Promise the Moon #1

Wolf at the Door #2

Over the Moon #3

Araneae Nation

A Heart of Ice #.5

A Hint of Frost #1

A Feast of Souls #2

A Cast of Shadows #2.5

A Time of Dying #3

A Kiss of Venom #3.5

A Breath of Winter #4

A Veil of Secrets #5

Daughters of Askara

Everlong #1

Evermine #2

Eversworn #3

Wicked Kin

Soul Weaver #1